WHO MURDERED REYNARD?

Borgo Press Books by S. Fowler Wright

Arresting Delia: An Inspector Cleveland Classic Crime Novel
The Attic Murder: An Inspector Combridge and Mr. Jellipot Classic Crime Novel
The Bell Street Murders: An Inspector Combridge and Mr. Jellipot Classic Crime Novel
Black Widow: A Classic Crime Novel
The Capone Caper: Mr. Jellipot vs. the King of Crime: A Classic Crime Novel
Crime & Co.: An Inspector Cleveland Classic Crime Novel
Dawn: A Novel of Global Warming
Dead by Saturday: An Inspector Cleveland Classic Crime Novel
The End of the Mildew Gang: An Inspector Cauldron Classic Crime Novel (Mildew Gang #3)
Four Callers in Razor Street: An Inspector Combridge and Mr. Jellipot Classic Crime Novel
The Hanging of Constance Hillier: An Inspector Cleveland Classic Crime Novel
The Jordans Murder: An Inspector Combridge and Mr. Jellipot Classic Crime Novel
The King Against Anne Bickerton: A Classic Crime Novel
The Mildew Gang: An Inspector Cauldron Classic Crime Novel (Mildew Gang #1)
Murder in Bethnal Square: An Inspector Combridge and Mr. Jellipot Classic Crime Novel
The Police and the Public
Post-Mortem Evidence: An Inspector Combridge and Mr. Jellipot Classic Crime Novel
The Return of the Mildew Gang: An Inspector Cauldron Classic Crime Novel (Mildew Gang #2)
The Rissole Mystery: An Inspector Combridge and Mr. Jellipot Classic Crime Novel
The Screaming Lake: A Lost Race Novel
The Secret of the Screen: An Inspector Combridge and Mr. Jellipot Classic Crime Novel
Three Witnesses: A Classic Crime Novel
Too Much for Mr. Jellipot: An Inspector Combridge and Mr. Jellipot Classic Crime Novel
The Vengeance of Gwa: A Fantasy of Prehistory
Was Murder Done? A Classic Crime Novel
Who Murdered Reynard? A Classic Crime Novel
The Wills of Jane Kanwhistle: An Inspector Combridge and Mr. Jellipot Classic Crime Novel
With Cause Enough?: An Inspector Combridge and Mr. Jellipot Classic Crime Novel

WHO MURDERED REYNARD?

A CLASSIC CRIME NOVEL

BEING A SEQUEL TO *THE BELL STREET MURDERS* AND *THE SECRET OF THE SCREEN*

by

S. FOWLER WRIGHT

WRITING AS "SYDNEY FOWLER"

The Borgo Press
An Imprint of Wildside Press LLC

MMVIII

CONTENTS

CHAPTER I.

Myra Is to Lie Well

"YOU SHOULD KNOW by this time, my dear Myra," Professor Blinkwell said easily, "that I have made it a rule of life that I take risks."

His niece delayed her reply while she put away another mouthful of the excellent bacon which the Professor had instructed her to order for breakfast, in preference to the rolls and coffee which the *Hôtel Splendide* usually served for the first meal of the day. Then she said, "I know how clever you are, and, of course, I've heard you say that before, but I can't see why you came over here while you might have stayed in London and kept clear of whatever trouble there is."

"That," the Professor replied, with the patient tolerance which he always showed towards his companion's intellectual inferiority, "is because you foolishly presume that danger is increased by proximity, or reduced by distance, whereas the fact may often be of a contrary kind.

"Where knowledge must be transmitted from mind to mind, it is well to observe that there is no form of communication that cannot be tapped, no code that cannot be read. There is one safe method alone—that of the open place and the whispered word."

It might be wrong to assume that Myra could not have followed her uncle's argument, had there been sufficient reason, but it is certain that she did not attempt to do so. She took no interest in the reflections of abstract wisdom, but held to her point in a woman's way.

"What I mean is, that if you'd stayed in London, it wouldn't have been your business at all. You've often told me that you've no concern with what happens until you hear that it's landed in England, and mayn't even know who handles it until then."

7

"That is true in the ordinary course. It is an organization in which curiosity is mutually undesirable, and is not encouraged by the head of the firm. But now that there is reason to think that something has gone wrong, and Gaspard being in jail—"

"I thought you said that that was on a charge of another kind?"

"So it is. We suppose it to have been faked, so that he can be kept under arrest at a time when his absence may be disastrous to us."

"And suppose they treat you in the same way?"

"My dear Myra! It would be an international outrage, which even the French police would be too shrewd, and too cautious, to try, even if such a thought should enter their heads, which it is not reasonable to suppose. What have I to do with the matters about which they fuss in this needless way, or what have they to do with me?"

Professor Blinkwell did not raise his voice, nor did his manner show any offence. His tone was that of good-humoured remonstrance against a preposterous suggestion.

But his niece was sensitive to the resentment which lay beneath the controlled suavity of a manner which seldom changed. She said: "Yes. I was silly, of course. But somehow I always feel safer in London than I do here."

"You are quite safe, if you take sufficient care to avoid the traffic of the busier streets."

"You know I didn't mean that."

"But I did. The French driving is of a peculiarly dangerous type. We kill each other in a stolid efficient manner, but they will run you down here with a *flair*, as taking pleasure in what they do."

Myra understood that her uncle intended to turn the conversation, which had developed a direction he did not approve though its subject was one on which he must speak frankly at times. She was the one person in the world who had his confidence in connection with the international drug trafficking of which he largely controlled the distribution in the British Isles, at least insofar as was necessary to enable her to act with intelligence in dealing with certain accounts through which it was contrived to manipulate the financial transactions involved, so that they should be innocent in their appearance to the banks concerned, and capable of plausible explanation if enquiry should be directed upon them.

Accepting the hint he gave, she spoke of that which had been on the surface of her mind before this conversation commenced. "I saw Will Kindell in the lounge yesterday evening. I suppose he's followed us here."

They both knew that she might have used the singular pronoun with greater accuracy, and the Professor, who was only vaguely aware of the existence of the young man she mentioned, and not always interested in her indecisive amours, became alertly curious.

"A young man of good family?"

"He's Lord Sparshott's cousin."

"And of good character, may we hope?"

"I should call him a bit soft."

"Of substantial means?"

"He hasn't a bean that he doesn't cadge."

"An unattractive type. But he has the good sense to be—shall we say, infatuated by what he thinks you to be?"

"Yes. Dotty. That's why he's here."

"And I may observe that his affections are not reciprocated with equal fervour?"

"It's just a bore to have to get out of his way."

The breakfast table became silent. Professor Blinkwell understood his niece very well, and she understood him, if not equally, at least better than most of his fellow creatures were able to do.

He knew that she was very unlikely to lose her head over Lord Sparshott's impecunious and apparently idle cousin, though her attitude towards him might not be entirely consistent with the boredom that she professed.

He knew that she liked to be flattered and stroked, like a well-fed cat, without caring overmuch whose hand might be smoothing her fur, and without desiring any more intimate association, or having the least intention of making return beyond the sound of a pleasant purr.

On her side she showed that she had followed her uncle's mind beyond anything which had been spoken aloud, when she broke the silence to add, "He's not the sort to be of any use to us, if you mean that."

"I wonder. He knows Thurlow, doesn't he? And Miss Thurlow, too?"

"Yes, he's a sort of English cousin to them. I don't know exactly what the relationship is. But I know that when they came to England they looked him up in the way Americans do."

"Well, that doesn't matter to us."

The breakfast table became silent again, and it was only as they were about to rise that Professor Blinkwell said: "You'd better not tire yourself trying to get out of his way. In fact, you'd better be as nice to him as you can contrive to be."

"May I ask why?"

After a moment's hesitation, the Professor, who had spoken in the act of rising, resumed his seat. He offered his cigarette case to his niece, and struck a match for their common use before he replied.

"Yes. I think you may. In fact, it may be necessary for you to know. Suppose," he went on, after a moment of thoughtful silence, "that you have some very valuable jewellery, of the existence of which I am unaware. Which could not come to my knowledge without grave embarrassment to yourself?"

"Yes?"

"You will be confronted with a difficult problem when we return to England in a few days' time. You will have to declare it to the Customs, and perhaps pay duty upon it, which you could hardly expect to do without my knowledge, or else take the risk of trying to smuggle it through."

As he said this, Professor Blinkwell observed a half-frightened, half-mutinous expression upon Myra's attractive, but rather heavy, features, which were not usually quick to expose her thoughts.

"I shouldn't like—" she began. "I didn't think you'd ever ask me to—"

"My dear Myra, don't be a fool! Are you supposing that you didn't think that you ever should?"

"I suppose you want me to ask Mr. Kindell to smuggle it through, without telling him what it is."

"Then you must think me a bigger fool than yourself. All you've got to do is to tell him about the trouble you're in. Do that within the next two days, but don't ask him to do any smuggling on your behalf, and don't agree to any offer that comes from him. For one reason, he'd be almost certain to fail; and there are two others that are even better than that."

As he spoke, the slightly sullen expression passed from his niece's face. She looked half puzzled and half relieved. She said: "Very well, I can do that, if it's any good."

"You can do it excellently, if you try, as I'm sure you will."

He rose again as he spoke, taking out a wallet at the same time, from which he drew some banknotes, which he handed to her.

"I suppose you'll want to go shopping now you're here," he said casually. "Most women do."

He paused at the door to add: "And don't forget that I never run any risks, and I shouldn't ask you to do anything that isn't perfectly safe. I've got too much to lose."

Myra heard these words with the relief which they had been intended to cause. They reminded her of the immunity with which

Professor Blinkwell had controlled the English traffic in certain illicit drugs for the past five years, without evidence of the faintest
suspicion being directed towards himself. Had he not told her more
than once before that she would never have cause to fear so long as
she obeyed his instructions with exactness, and without questioning
what they meant? And had not this assurance always been justified
by the event

The tale he had asked her to tell now was certainly not of a dangerous kind. Even had it been true, there could be no legal offence in
advance of an overt act.

She looked at the banknotes she had received and saw that they
amounted to a total of two thousand francs. She was pleased at that,
but she saw by the magnitude of the bribe that her uncle attached
unusual importance to the part he had asked her to play, however
safe it might be.

Well, it was not one she was likely to bungle! She remained
thoughtful for the next ten minutes, and then picked up the telephone and asked to be put through to Mr. Kindell's apartment.

CHAPTER II.

OF THOSE ON THE FLOOR ABOVE

WHILE PROFESSOR BLINKWELL and his niece discussed business, finance, and matters which might be designated by a more sinister word, Mr. Cyril B. Thurlow, United States Ambassador to the Court of St. James, and his daughter Irene, were consuming an equally satisfactory breakfast of grapefruit and shredded wheat in their own suite on the floor above.

Mr. Thurlow, whose name had been prominent two years before as a possible candidate for the United States presidency, but who had withdrawn in favour of a more popular candidate, had been subsequently appointed—in recognition of the party loyalty which he had shown and other excellent qualifications—to the office which he now held.

Having secured that exalted position, he had maintained its high traditions to the satisfaction of the nations concerned, and was seldom absent from his official residence in London; but on this occasion, the political skies being clear, and there being a sufficient interval during which no ceremonial functions would require his presence, he had left his official duties in the hands of capable secretaries, and followed inclination and his daughter's wishes by making a short visit to Paris.

Mr. Thurlow was an Alabama cotton planter of substantial wealth and assured social position. He was known as a man of something more than superficial scholarship, as a collector of medieval tapestries, and as one of the three best after-dinner speakers of his race and generation.

He had shown another side of his character, and had greatly increased his popularity with his fellow citizens, five years before when he had come suddenly upon three men who were in the act of kidnapping his daughter, in accordance with one of the best known customs of his native land.

Declining the usual invitation to raise his hands, he had pulled out his own gun with such celerity, and used it to such effect, that the police had been subsequently called upon to do no more than remove one dying and two seriously wounded men, while his own injuries had been confined to a grazed cheek and an abbreviation of the little finger of the left hand, which had been shot off at the upper joint.

He spoke excellent English, with a slight, pleasant Southern-States drawl; and though he insisted on pronouncing schedule with a "K," for which authority can be advanced, it is improbable that he ever expressed approval of a fellow man by describing him as a swell guy.

His daughter Irene, a vivaciously attractive, rather impulsive girl of nineteen or twenty years, an only and motherless child, had left college at her own urging, and to his own satisfaction, when he had been appointed to his present position, so that she could accompany him to England.

On arriving in that country, she had made it a primary occupation to discover descendants of her Father's Scottish ancestors, or living relatives of her mother, who was traditionally connected with the Shropshire Charlings.

In this pursuit she had done no more for her father than to identify his family with that of an Alexander Thurlow, who was the proprietor of a general store in a small village near Haddington. The man was of dubious character and less than dubious sobriety, and the relationship had been left unclaimed, after her father's inclinations had been expressed with as much freedom of emphasis as he would often allow himself to use in his daughter's presence.

But she had been more successful, at least to her own, if not to the ambassador's, mind in her search for her mother's kin. They proved to be numerous, of a good average respectability, and including some of more than average social status. Considered broadly, they were a family in which charm of manner and speech, a resilient optimism, and an opportunist ability to avoid the impact of adverse circumstance, were conspicuous above the more solid and pedestrian virtues, though it would be uncharitable to suggest that these may not have been also present.

Among them, William Kindell, cousin of Lord Sparshott, who had been living in London with more evidence of leisure than occupation, had shown some disposition to accept the generous Embassy hospitality which Mr. Thurlow had offered to the family of his dead wife, and which he had lacked excuse to withdraw when he had observed, with some inward dissatisfaction, that the young man ap-

13

peared to be gaining an exceptional measure of his daughter's regard; especially as he could not detect anything in his conduct either open to criticism in itself or suggesting that he regarded Irene with more than the friendliness natural to their ages and dispositions, and to the blood relationship that existed between them.

Now Irene broke a short silence to ask, in the pseudo-casual voice of one who is self-conscious of speaking too often on a subject which fills the mind, and yet cannot resist the inclination to do so, "Did you notice that Will Kindell's been here since yesterday?" To which he answered with a vague illogical feeling of grievance (for the *Hôtel Splendide* was equally open to all who dressed in the right way, avoided public disgrace, and could pay its bills): "Kindell? I wonder whatever he's doing here. I suppose he's not following us?"

Irene would have liked to feel that the supposition was wrong, but she had some reluctant reason for a different opinion. She said: "No, I don't think he knows we're here. It's more likely to be something to do with a Professor Blinkwell, or some name like that, on the floor below. I saw him talking last night to the Professor's daughter—unless she's his wife—a fat, Jewish-looking woman, but he didn't notice me as I passed."

The ambassador surprised himself by saying, "Well, if he's staying here, you'd better ask him to look us up."

He spoke from mingled, unanalysed feelings which pulled contrary ways. He was naturally hospitable, and unlikely to fail in friendly offices towards a kinsman in a strange city. He had a clear perception that the permission would please Irene, to do which was always his first aim. He did not wish the young man, for whom he had only moderate liking, to become too attractive to her; but he had an unreasonable feeling of resentment at the idea that William Kindell might not value that which he did not mean him to have. If Irene should show liking for him, it would be intolerable for him to give preference to Professor Blinkwell's niece!

He thought he detected, beyond the fact, a tone of hostile jealousy in Irene's description of the lady in question. Like many men of spare frame, he had a tendency to admire women of the more fleshy types, and Myra might have had some just cause for annoyance had she known that anyone called her fat. A controlled plumpness, equally due to laziness, good living, and a placidity of conscience such as is possible only to those who can do evil without regret, would be a fairer description of the curves to which the ambassador had paid the tribute of an admiring glance as he had passed her upon the stairs. But to Irene, subconscious of her own lithe slimness and her ten-year advantage of youth, fat was the fitting word.

Irene hesitated in her reply, the simplicity of her desire for her cousin's company warring against the feminine instinct that aims less to pursue than attract pursuit. "I don't think," she said, "I'll call him up if he doesn't know that we're here. I expect we shall run across him somewhere."

"Yes," her father agreed dryly, "I'd say we shall."

He rose up from the breakfast table saying that he had some correspondence with which to deal, but no more than could be cleared off in a couple of hours. After that, perhaps an early lunch, and then where would she like to go?

Irene said she would think it over. Her father retired to his own room, and left her to a thoughtful solitude, similar to that of Myra on the floor below.

And meanwhile William Kindell, the common subject of these two very different conversations, having breakfasted in the more expeditious manner of those whom conversation does not divert, had strolled into the smoking room to pick up a paper which he did not read, while his thoughts dwelt upon the two young women who had been talking of him.

It was true that he had not seen Irene when she had passed him the evening before, but he knew that she was there, having signed the hotel register immediately below the entry of Cyril B. Thurlow and his daughter. The information would have been more welcome had he not come in pursuit of another girl, and seen also the possibility that his appearance might be misinterpreted, in the absence of an explanation he could not give.

He liked Irene, as, indeed, it was easy to do. Had his position been free, when they had first met, her own ready liking for him might have wakened a warmer response. But that was only a few days after his introduction to Myra Blinkwell, and the commencement of a flirtation which appeared to have been stimulated rather than cooled by her own lazily good-humoured indifference.

Myra might say little and do less, but she was one of those women whose physical appearance suggests (perhaps delusively), a voluptuousness of passion which is waiting to be awakened, like a fire unlit, but which has been generously laid with piling of ample logs.

CHAPTER III.

MYRA GOES INTO ACTION

WILLIAM KINDELL was known to have a small income which had been settled upon him by a relative, on an impulse of exceptional family prudence, in such a way that it was beyond his creditors' reach. Apart from that, he appeared to have no regular occupation, and no financial resources beyond what he could gain by backing his considerable wits against those of the professional bookmaker or the banker of the baccarat table.

He had thus some measure of freedom for the pursuit of whatever might attract attention or rouse desire, and when Myra, whether casually or deliberately, had mentioned that she would be accompanying Professor Blinkwell to Paris (which Mrs. Blinkwell, being a nervous invalid, was unwilling to do), it had required no more than a few hours to enable him to provide himself with an excuse for travelling in the same direction.

He might not wish to advertise to the whole world that it was the attraction of Myra Blinkwell which had caused that hurried journey to be undertaken, but he was not unwilling that she, at least, should be able to make a good guess. The fact that he had come in pursuit of one lady may have made him quicker to see that he might be judged in the same way in a direction he had not meant; and it implied neither unfriendliness to Irene, nor ingratitude for the hospitality he had received from her father's hands, that the difficulty of putting himself in the way of one fellow guest at the hotel, while keeping out of the sight of another, was the dilemma which he now considered.

He was in funds at the moment, having backed *Pilgrim's Progress* rather heavily a fortnight before, when the odds had been exceptionally good; and he was not one who held tightly to the money that fortune gave. He went through life bringing subordinates to his service with liberal tips, and the first thought that came to him now was that a ten-franc note would obtain the number of the Blinkwells' suite, without the necessity for a personal enquiry at the hotel bureau; and a more substantial outlay would discover the nearest vacant room with a similar discretion.

After that, it would be a simple matter to make some excuse for being transferred to a position in which he could meet the girl he sought, in the corridor or upon the stairs, with little risk of the encounter which he would prefer to avoid.

He had come to this resolution, and was in the act of beckoning for a boy who would have been commissioned to undertake the first part of the programme, when his purpose was arrested by the sight of Myra standing in the gap of the open door.

Her eyes glanced over a dozen other occupants of the room to fall upon himself, at which they gave a look of pleased, rather surprised recognition, and she came directly towards him.

"I am looking," she explained, "for Professor Blinkwell. I suppose you haven't seen him anywhere about?"

She might not have felt it necessary to make so direct or prompt an approach had not the gentleman she professed to seek returned to the breakfast room a few minutes before, and said, with an emphasis he rarely employed: "It's no use sitting here. When I ask you to do anything, I don't want it delayed. I want you to act at once."

To which Myra, who was not easy to hurry, either in physical or mental movements, had replied reasonably: "Why, you only asked me ten minutes ago! You didn't say there was such a hurry as that. And I haven't lost any time at all. I've tried to ring him up in his room, but he isn't there. I was just thinking how to make up the tale in a natural way."

As she spoke, she perceived that her uncle's reproach had not only been unreasonable in itself, which, coming from him, was a sufficiently surprising circumstance, but that it had been spoken in a manner as near to perturbation as she had ever seen him exhibit. The few minutes that he had been absent had been spent in his writing room, which opened out of the one they were in and had no other entrance. Almost certainly he had been alone the whole time. What could have occurred to cause him to talk to her in such a way? Even for him (or rather, for all the money that he was likely to give), she did not intend to run any risk of being arrested on a criminal charge. She said inconsequently, "I don't think you ought to ask me to do things without explaining what they're about."

But while she spoke Professor Blinkwell had recovered whatever of his usual suave urbanity may have been momentarily lost.

"I'm afraid," he said, "I gave rather a jolt to your mental processes before your rather ample breakfast had settled down. But the fact is that I have just recollected that there is a board meeting of the Purling Chemical Company on Thursday which it is important for me to attend, so that we must get back to London almost at once.

"But as to what I've asked you to do, it's a simple matter that can't make trouble under any circumstances. Even if Kindell should give you away, which you know quite well that he wouldn't do, and if his tale were believed (and it wouldn't sound very probable when there's no such jewellery to be found), you couldn't be charged with any offence that is known to the French law. He couldn't say that you'd done more than talk about doing something wrong, and even that would have no more than his unsupported word against ours, which is quite as good."

"Yes, I see that, but I don't understand—"

"And it isn't necessary that you should. If I want you to do anything further, I'll explain then, which will be the best time. But I want you to get it into your head that neither you nor I are going to risk anything over this affair. We're not going to be in it at all."

"Well," she said, rising in a slow and rather sullen reluctance under the force of his stronger will, "if there's such a rush, I'd better see if I can find him anywhere now. I don't want to have to ring up his room again."

She did not believe the tale of the board meeting, and she had an instinctive perception of the fact that her uncle was in nearer danger than he would admit to her, or perhaps to his own mind.

But she had confidence still in his ability to avoid it, well founded on past experience, and she could not answer his argument that there was, as yet, little aspect of danger to herself in that which he had asked her to do.

As to any development in his own affairs which could have disturbed his mind since his request had been made half an hour before, it is a fact that he had been alone in his room for the whole of the intervening period, occupied in the writing of a quite innocent business letter, and interrupted only by a telephone call which, on the evidence both of himself and the angry Frenchman at the other end of the line, had not been intended for him. M. Bonfleur had been urgent in his desire to inform the Messieurs Céleste et Cie that a consignment of Spanish grapes must be taken off his hands by 5:00 P.M. tomorrow if legal consequences were to be avoided. He had been in a state of angry and voluble excitement which had made it difficult for the Professor to convince him that he had been put through to the wrong number, and he had expressed and repeated his facts and feelings with much unnecessary emphasis before admitting his mistake, and checking, abruptly, with a curt apology, and a more elaborate curse upon the inefficiency of the telephone service.

"No," Kindell replied, "I don't think he's been here. Not since I came in some time ago."

"Then I don't know where he can be. I've looked about every-where else."

"Perhaps, if you wait here, he might—"

"Yes, I dare say that's as good a chance as running around," she said doubtfully. "We might only miss each other again." Hesitantly, she sat down and accepted a cigarette, her eyes still watching the door.

"Nothing that I can do for you?" he asked hopefully, thanking Fate for that which had the appearance of better fortune than he could reasonably have expected.

"No, thanks. I'm only going shopping, but I thought I'd get him to go with me, if he hadn't anything special on this morning. He talks the language a lot better than I do."

"You know Paris?"

"I've never been here before."

"Then, if Professor Blinkwell isn't available, may I offer to show you round?"

"Oh, no," she said, but in a more gracious tone than he had ex-pected to hear. "I couldn't ask you to do that. You'd get bored to death. I might stay in one shop for hours! Besides I don't suppose it will be more than two minutes before my uncle turns up."

William Kindell could not regard this as a very hopeful reply, but did not accept rebuff. He said: "Oh, but you're wrong there! There's nothing I should like more."

He said this with a sincerity which was sufficiently evident but Myra, remembering a coolness she had shown him at their last meet-ing in London, was too adroit to accept the proffered service now. She said: "It's very nice of you to say that. But I've no doubt you've got your own business to do. You haven't come to Paris to waste time showing me round the shops!"

He was sufficiently skilful in such exchanges to avoid the obvi-ous denial which would have sounded as no more than a perfunctory courtesy. He said: "Oh, well, it's always better to expect a little and get a lot. I only came to look up a man who owes me a betting debt, as I happened to hear he was in funds and it would be the right time to touch him for the amount. I can get ahold of him best at night, so I'm quite free now."

His voice and manner dismissed the defaulting debtor into the category of trivial things. They suggested more convincingly than direct assertion might have done that she had been the real lure that had brought him there. As she remained noncommittally silent, and the gesture with which she crushed out the end of her cigarette indicated that at the next moment she might be rising to go, he added, "Suppose you give Professor Blinkwell another two minutes, and if he hasn't turned up by then, you make the best of me for a substitute?"

She appeared to hesitate at this, and said at last: "It's very kind of you, if you really mean it. But I'm not dressed to go out, so we can give him longer than that. I shall be down in about ten minutes, and if he hasn't appeared by then, I shall suppose he's forgotten me altogether. So if he comes in while I'm upstairs perhaps you'd ask him to wait."

Mr. Kindell undertook this, and she went back to her own rooms to warn the Professor not to go down until she had left the hotel, and to prepare herself for the expedition during the next half hour, which was as punctual to the promised ten minutes as a woman could be expected to be.

CHAPTER IV.

MYRA SEEKS ADVICE

MYRA SHOPPED WITH discrimination, and the economy of effort which her disposition preferred, and even a man less infatuated than William Kindell appeared to be would not have found attendance upon her to be a very arduous or boring task.

She was not one of those women who turn over a hundred articles and remain in a condition of bewildered indecision as to what, if anything, they desire to purchase. Her usual method was to examine the shop windows, and occasionally to fasten upon some article which she would acquire, not without some shrewdness of bargaining in her indolent way, but with a fixed intention of having it at the best price she could, be it low or high. That was no more than her normal manner, but in this case her primary object was of another kind.

At eleven-thirty she required coffee. At twelve-fifty-five she consented graciously to a suggestion of lunch.

During the course of the meal, a discussion of her purchases led very naturally to the question of what duty she would have to pay to the English Customs upon them. She said that she had had no trouble coming out.

"No," he said, "you wouldn't be likely to have much, if you only brought your own things."

"I heard someone say it's much worse going back."

"You mean the English Customs are worse than the French? I should say no to that. Rather the other way. But, of course, if you come over and buy things here, the trouble comes when you're getting them home. Not that it ought to be any trouble to you. You don't want to smuggle anything. It wouldn't be worth your while."

"No. Of course not. But I don't see how they can find out if anyone really plans to get some jewellery through. Suppose a woman hid a diamond ring in her dress? They don't search people. Not most of them, anyway."

"No, but I believe they're very good at guessing who to suspect. Though I've no doubt they get it done at times. They've got a good many ways of checking up that the public don't know. I believe a lot of the shop assistants here are bribed to report purchases by foreign visitors, so that the Customs officers know just what to look for before they start."

"It seems rather a mean thing to do."

"But I don't think that would apply to such purchases as you made this morning. They weren't very costly, and you spread them out over several shops. All the same, I should say you'd do the wise thing if you declare them carefully."

"Of course I shall...I wasn't thinking of them. You can't be charged duty on anything you brought out of England, if you're just taking it back?"

"No, you can be quite sure about that."

"Even if you didn't declare it when you came out?"

William Kindell did not answer this conundrum directly. He had wits enough to perceive that he was not merely asked his opinion on an abstract question. He said, "Perhaps I could advise you better if you would tell me just what the trouble is."

"I have got some things I didn't declare. I couldn't very well without Uncle knowing I'd got them with me, which there was a reason against, and I shan't want to going back."

Kindell looked puzzled. "It wasn't very wise to bring them under those circumstances, was it?"

"No, perhaps not, but it's done now. I thought I might go to places where I could wear them—times when he wouldn't be coming along."

"And now you're getting worried as to how you'll get them back?"

"Yes. I thought you might think of something. You know more about how these things are arranged."

"I'm afraid I can't claim—"

"If you wanted to, I think you'd be certain to find a way."

"How soon are you going back?"

"Almost at once. There's a wretched meeting Uncle's got to attend."

"I think, if I were you, I'd go to the Customs here, and tell them just what the facts are. You'd probably be able to prove that whatever it is—jewellery? Well, I might have guessed that—was bought in England, and whether they make you pay duty or not, you could arrange to send them home by registered post."

Myra showed no pleasure at this prospect. "I thought you'd think of something a lot better than that."

"Well, perhaps I shall. I'll let you know if I do."

It was an assurance that won him her sweetest smile. "I knew," she said, assuming much more than he had said, "that you'd think of something to get me out of the mess."

She shook her head in smiling rejection of his protest that she must not be too confident of his power to help her, however willing he might be.

She turned the conversation to more personal directions as they drove back to the hotel, being more familiar in her lazy sensuous manner than he had found her before.

On arriving, they parted at the lift door, she going up to her uncle's suite, after he had accepted her invitation to join them for the English tea which the Professor required to be served to him at 4:00 P.M., in whatever country he might honour with his distinguished presence.

She went up to announce that she had accomplished what she had been told to do, and received the expected praise. Her digestive processes might have worked less smoothly had she been able to hear the conversation which was proceeding in one of the telephone booths on the ground floor. "I think," Kindell was saying, "they're trying to make me a stooge to smuggle the stuff through. But I'll see you tonight. I may know a bit more then."

Coming out of the booth, he met Irene, and accepted the invitation which she gave in her father's name that he should join them that night at dinner. She would have been better pleased had he not added that he might have to leave almost immediately afterwards. He did not mention the evasive debtor of whom he had told Myra, but he said he might have business which he could not defer.

Irene, who had assumed that an acceptance of the invitation would imply an evening among the pleasure resorts of a city which had so much gaiety to offer to the visitor whose purse was sufficiently plenished, allowed her disappointment to show for one short second before she answered, with her usual friendly tone: "Oh well, of course, if you must. *Les affaires sont les affaires.*"

She went up to tell her father that she had given the invitation he had proposed, and how it had been received. Had she, she wondered, been incredibly snubbed? Did he mean that he would dine with her father, but did not intend to risk having to spend subsequent time with her? She put the idea resolutely from a generous mind.

CHAPTER V.

AN UNOPENED PARCEL

IT MAY BE that whatever the enigmatic telephone call had required Professor Blinkwell to arrange before 5:00 P.M. tomorrow had been accomplished when Myra returned to lunch, for he met her in his usual mood of cheerful complacency and praised her for what she had done. He would be pleased, he said, and at leisure, to meet Kindell at four for tea.

"I don't see," she answered, "that I've done much yet, nor what I'm supposed to be going to do."

"My dear Myra! Can you not leave that to me to judge? If I am pleased, you may be content that you have done well. There is a parcel on my desk. Will you secrete it somewhere now, and show it to him this afternoon, when I am not about, as containing the articles which you must conceal? I will provide you with opportunity to do that. But do not give it to him today. I do not wish it to pass into his hands until you are on the point of leaving tomorrow. It is possible that I may not be able to go myself till the next day."

Whatever pleasure Myra may have shown at the commencement of this speech gave way to a mutinous frown as its later purport penetrated her mind. Had she not had his explicit promise that she should not be directly involved in the handling of these illicit drugs? Was it not, apart from that, contrary to the basic rule of his own conduct, the wisdom of which he had so often impressed upon her lazily receptive mind? And at a time when suspicion of complicity in such trafficking had approached him more nearly than they believed it had ever done before! And the parcel in their own room! There was excuse for the sullen rebellious pout that emphasized the heaviness of her lips as she protested, "You can't ask me to do that! You've told me ever so many times—"

The Professor interrupted her with his usual suavity, but with an inflection in his voice which she knew to be a sign of rising anger not to be lightly provoked: "If I've told you ever so many times, there should be no occasion to do so again. You should have learnt by now that I mean what I say, neither more nor less."

It may be thought that if Myra, knowing Professor Blinkwell's occupations and moral code as she did, could think him incapable of a lying assurance, she must have been of a peculiar intellectual density, but there was reason behind his words.

It would not have occurred to either of them to tell the truth if they should have seen use in a lie. To do so would have seemed as foolish as to walk through a pool of water when a side-step would find drier ground. But because your comrade carries an offensive weapon, it does not follow that he will make a habit of sticking it into your own back.

Lying, like liars, differs. Much of it is no better (nor worse) than the poor shield of the weak. With some it may reach the degradation of habit, against which even friendship is not secure. With such, even the abject defensive value of it may be largely lost, for what is the power of a lie which is not believed? And as true words must be weighed in the same scale of discredit, those who fall so far become naked to every wind.

But there are others to whom the lie is a weapon for cool and deliberate use. Having learnt its deadliness in efficient lips, they do not give it light or promiscuous exercise, nor use it so that it must destroy confidence in themselves where it is important that it should remain. Honour among thieves is no empty phrase. It is of the necessity which is above law.

Myra knew her uncle to be cunning and ruthless, a man of heartless criminalities, with no scruples at all. But she had found that what he promised would be performed; what he told her would happen, did. Now he had told her that he would not deviate from the rule that neither she nor he should have any part in the smuggling of the illicit drugs from which his fortune was made, and asked her to believe this, even while the parcel was in the room, and they were plotting together to procure Kindell to pass it through the English Customs in his own luggage. With a half-bewildered, half-resentful mind, she yet bent to habit and experience, and the influence of a will more powerful if not more obstinate than her own. She said sullenly: "Well, I don't know what to believe when you say two things at once. They're not sense. But I'll show him the parcel, if that's all you want me to do. What shall I say if he asks to see what's inside?"

"My dear Myra! Are you a child? If you can't handle him in such a little matter as that—! And I've told you he's only to see that you've got it ready, and that you'll want him to take charge of it to-morrow. He needn't touch it at all."

"But he'd have to tomorrow. And besides—"

"Myra, I sometimes think you're a fool. If he's coaxed into smuggling your parcel through, do you suppose that he'll want to *know* that it's full of things he ought to declare?"

"Well, I don't like doing it. That's a fact."

"You make that quite plain. But we all have to do things we don't like at times. And if you do just what I've told you—as I'm quite sure you will—you'll have nothing to worry over. Nothing at all."

With these words they parted to their own rooms, and, when four o'clock and William Kindell came, Myra did her allotted part, as her uncle had been sure that she would.

When he left the room, she showed the parcel, which she produced from beneath the head cushion of a couch on which she had disposed herself with some exhibition of shapely limbs. She said, "I don't want to bother you with it now, but I thought you'd like to see that it isn't a dreadful size," assuming that it was agreed between them that he would give her the help she asked.

"Perhaps," he said, watching her more closely than she was aware, and in another mood than that which she wished to rouse, "if you'd let me declare them among my own things, the duty wouldn't be such a lot to pay."

"No, indeed," she exclaimed, quickly controlling the startled note in her voice, "I couldn't possibly let you do that, especially when everyone knows how—"

She stopped abruptly. She was about to end with "how poor you are," and recognized, somewhat late, that they were words which politeness might not approve. But the suggestion was one for which she had been unprepared, and her uncle's readiness was not hers. She concluded, "No, I couldn't possibly let you do that."

He might have replied, with less courtesy than truth, that he had not proposed that he should, but only asked whether it would be a large sum; but he responded easily, "Well, it's for you to say," and was paid with a grateful glance from lazily seductive eyes.

It may be said that both of them acted well.

CHAPTER VI.

The Methods of Henri Reynard

KINDELL'S DINNER WITH the Thurlows was not an entire success, for which there were more causes than one.

Had he been directly asked, he would not have denied that the Blinkwells had entertained him for tea, but he was unaware that Irene had happened to see him enter the suite on the floor below, and that her father had seen him leave more than an hour and a half later. Following a morning spent with Myra among Paris shops, this seemed to suggest a degree of intimacy which exceeded fact, and its apparent significance was not lessened when an allusion was made to which he might have replied more frankly had he guessed how much was already known. As it was, his reticence gave the event a false importance, different from, if not greater than, that which it really had.

With no entirely convincing reason for his withdrawal, he left almost as soon as dinner was over, both host and hostess dismissing him with a degree of coolness he had not experienced previously. Irene was vexed by the doubt which is more fretting than certainty. Her father felt the resentment of one whose hospitality is casually received, and, more consciously, of one whose daughter is too lightly esteemed.

Besides that, he had a quick sympathy with Irene's feelings, the understanding between them having the closeness which will come of single association. It led him, before Kindell had reached the lift, to the irritable exclamation:

"What, in the name of Satan, the young fool can see in that coarse-faced Jewess—"

To which Irene aware of implications her pride would not consent to see, replied lightly: "Oh, I don't know! There's a lot of men who don't like short weight in a wife. But I'd say she'll cost him something to keep."

His mind very far from any question of feeding Myra, either as a wife or in any other capacity, Kindell walked sharply to the next corner, and stood there until a vehicle drew up at the pavement. It was a taxi for public hire, but no word passed between him and the driver as he got in, and he left it, half an hour later, in the same manner, without tendering or being asked for a fare.

He alighted in a quiet road opposite a small gate that broke the line of a high dark hedge, and walked, as one who had been before, up a straight path that lengthened narrowly beneath meeting boughs, crossed a wide lawn, and came to the back of a house, isolated in its own grounds, which showed a solitary obscured light at the ground floor level.

Making straight to this, he tapped a short Morse signal on the French window, which promptly opened a sufficient space to admit him.

Blinking in the bright light as the window curtains fell into place, he shook hands with a short, rather plump Frenchman, who greeted him with an official brusqueness which was habit, and a courtesy of more personal kind.

With an abrupt gesture he directed his guest to a fireside chair opposite his own. He indicated wine and cigars on a low table at Kindell's side. Almost at the same instant his words turned to the business upon their minds.

His glance, bright and sharp, read Kindell's face as he asked: "You bring news? You will land the fish?"

He spoke in English, of which he had idiomatic control, only accent and an occasional idiosyncrasy of construction showing that he was using a foreign tongue.

"Yes. That's how it looks to me."

Concisely but fully, Kindell told of Myra's request, and of the parcel which she had asked him to take to England.

Henri Reynard, normally an excitable and voluble man, could control his speech at the right times. Had it been otherwise, he would not have risen to be a departmental head of the Bureau de Sûreté, nor would he have been the police official of all Europe most dreaded by the international criminals it was his special business to foil and catch.

Now he listened with silent, concentrated attention till the tale was told. Then he asked, but not as one who is interested in the reply: "You think it is as simple as that? Well, who knows!" He became silent, gnawing a moustache which seemed a size too large for its owner's mouth, as his habit was. He muttered, *"Toujours la femme,"* but not as one to whom conviction easily came.

Kindell saw that his narrative had roused doubt rather than satisfaction. He answered: "Well, that's what the facts are. It looks a walkover now to me, unless they get frightened and jib. If you think that's likely, I suppose it would be better to raid them at once, while the parcel's there. But I don't see why they should. They must have been very sure of me before—"

His words ceased as he saw that Reynard was giving little attention as he chewed the doubt in his own mind. Kindell thought the little Frenchman to be theatrical in his manners, and over-elaborate in his methods.

He thought the way in which they met to be of a melodramatic quality beyond anything which the occasion required. English police methods, he would have said, are no less effective because they move along straighter paths. But he knew Reynard's reputation, and paid him the respect which achievements earn. He became silent also, until the French police officer gave him a belated reply.

"Raid Blinkwell's suite now? But I should say not! If they really trust you, it would be a rotten mistake; and a lot worse if they don't. No, we must go on. Let the woman know that you'll see her through, and fall in with her own plans. That shouldn't be hard to do."

There was nothing discourteous in this, either in words or tone, but there came an uneasy doubt to Kindell's mind. Was there an underlying sarcasm, as though Reynard thought that hard things were beyond his power? It seemed undeserved. So far he had done all that he had been asked and had reported success.

Reynard asked abruptly, "Blinkwell knows you're a friend of the Thurlows?"

"Yes. I believe he does. Myra knows."

"And she hasn't asked you to use them for this?"

"No, it hasn't been mentioned at all."

"Well, there's time yet."

"You mean that the Thurlows' baggage wouldn't be opened?"

Reynard was precise. "They are not entitled to take anything dutiable through our Customs because he is an ambassador to a third Power, but it is extremely unlikely that they would attempt any serious smuggling, and their declarations would normally be accepted without much interference, if any, with the contents of their trunks. Going *back* to England, it is unlikely that they would be challenged."

"But I suppose that mine would be examined in the usual way? It seems to me that they are taking a great risk."

"Yes, you see that." (Was there sarcasm in this wording again? It was hard to say.)

"Of course, they may think that I shouldn't be under suspicion, and more likely—"

"Then they must think they are under no suspicion themselves. Otherwise, having been associated with them—"

"Still, if they're cornered, it may be the best they can do."

"Yes," Reynard agreed; "we must hope it is." But there was no conviction in his voice.

"Anyhow, I'm to carry on, even if I'm to be the fool of the piece?"

A gleam of appreciative humour came into the Frenchman's eyes. His thought was—how hard it is to tell how dull these stolid English actually are! He said cordially, "Oh, but you won't be that! You do your part well."

Kindell got up to go, but learnt that he would have to stay ten minutes longer, after which he must walk away from the gate, taking a left-hand way, until a taxi should pick him up, as, at that time, it would be certain to do. Well, everyone to his own methods! With a word of polite recognition of the precautions with which the secrecy of his movements was guarded, he accepted the plan.

CHAPTER VII.

MONSIEUR REYNARD CONTRIVES A CRIME

FEW PEOPLE HAVE sleepless nights, and even to those few, the experience seldom comes. But if a man wake at intervals to concentrate an alert mind on a problem that has baffled him during the day, and those intervals occupy even a quarter of the night hours, he may scarcely be conscious of having slept. And those sleep-divided oases of thought may often be more fruitful both of decision and design than the most wakeful hours of the day.

Henri Reynard had been engaged for the past two years in a duel which he had not won—so far was he from his goal that he had only recently been able to make a good guess of whom his principal opponents were. Now he had progressed so far that he was assured of several names, of whom Professor Blinkwell, an Englishman of international scientific reputation, was not the least. He was so sure of Blinkwell that, had it been in his power to sentence him without trial, he would have done it in the certainty of a just deed. But suspicion, however strong, is not proof, of which he owned to himself that he had none. Scotland Yard, which had first suggested Blinkwell as the probable head of the English operations of the gang, had to admit the same difficulty. Now, the fact that Blinkwell had come to Paris confirmed these presumptions. But in itself, it was of no evidential value. To visit Paris was not a crime.

Yet the hunt was up. A large parcel of illicit drugs, designed to be realized at a huge profit among English addicts, had been nearly seized. The channels used for conveying previous parcels to England had been blocked. Beyond that, the places for secure hiding in Paris had been exposed. It had become precarious to keep it longer in Paris, and perilous to attempt its transit to England. And now the temptation to attempt that transit must be extreme; for the English police admitted frankly that, if it could not be seized *en route*, they had no clue to the hands into which it would afterwards pass. The closer the Paris hunt, the more arrests that were made, the stronger the inducement would be to take the path, however perilous, at the end of which both profit and safety lay. And now Blinkwell, departing, it seemed, from his usual aloofness, had come himself to oversee, if not to conduct, the operations which the occasion required.

M. Reynard's wakeful hours, it might be thought, would be engaged upon subtle plans for trapping the man of whose guilt he was so confidently assured. But this idea would be wrong. Through the night hours he was Professor Blinkwell, not a chief of Paris police. Ceaselessly, he contrived plans to baffle the Customs officers, casting them aside, one by one, as he saw their flaws. "I must think," he told himself time after time, "of something better than that." It was near the dawn when he passed into peaceful sleep with the thought that he had a solution at last. "It is simple," he told himself. "It is about the simplest plan I have had. But it may be the better for that."

CHAPTER VIII.

The Misadventure of a False Bottom

MYRA WAS PLAINLY nervous. She looked at Kindell with troubled, questioning eyes. She asked: "You really think you will get it through?"

She had had an angry enigmatic contest with her uncle, who had given assurances which appeared to be inconsistent with that which, in the same breath, he required her to do; and which had ended in his telling her that she talked too much, and it was no use her trying to use brains that she hadn't got, and that she must trust his judgment, or go back to England to find another home than she now had.

"Do you think, my dear Myra," he had asked, "I should entrust anything to you which you might muck? Don't I know that you would give me away in a moment if you thought that you were in the slightest danger from the police which you could ward off in no other way? When you say I'm asking you to do a dangerous thing, you simply call me a fool."

The smoothness of his quiet voice had not concealed from her the anger with which he spoke. She cared nothing for the imputations on her own brains, which she had heard often before, but fear made her stubborn as she replied: "I can't see why you won't tell me plainly what it all means. Everyone likes to understand what they do."

"Which is precisely the position in which I have placed you now. You have only to do what you are told—and even you are not stupid enough to go wrong in that—and you'll have nothing to fear. As a matter of fact, I can tell you this: the Customs will pass anything Kindell carries with no trouble at all."

"You mean it's an arranged thing?"

"I mean just what I have said, neither more nor less. When you're in England, you can take the parcel back from him, and keep it till I return, and if you've got any use for a hundred pounds, I'll give you a note of that value when I see you again. But that's on condition that I have no more sulky nonsense to hear, for I've got things of more importance to do."

Sulky or not, she had become silent at that, but she was only half assured, and her nervousness was plain for Kindell to see.

He answered confidently. "Yes, it will be all right. See what I've brought."

He opened a small suitcase, such as would be easy to handle. He showed a false bottom, of a size which proved to be sufficient for the parcel which lay between them. That was well. She had feared, as he spoke, that she would be required to open and repack it. She was in a puzzled doubt as to what it would show, but she was sure that her uncle would not thank her for that.

He said: "You needn't worry. You needn't even be near me. But anyway, I shall get it through."

He spoke with literal accuracy. Whatever the parcel might contain, her trouble was meant to be at a later hour. He was to be passed through the Customs with light inspection, by an arrangement the police had made, and then return the parcel to Myra. After that, they would part, and what would happen then would be beyond his knowledge or control. Actually, she was to be shadowed by members of the C.I.D., who would either arrest her with the packet still in her possession or let her go to do with it what she would. The alternatives were to depend upon a wire from the Bureau de Sûreté, which Reynard had undertaken to send so that it would arrive at about the same time as they. Such was the plan which he had proposed in a telephone discussion between his department and the headquarters of the C.I.D., which had become heated at times, as he had insisted on his own way with less adequate explanation than his colleagues thought they were entitled to have. Did they want, he asked, to alarm the Blinkwells by arresting Myra on a minor charge? Did they want Kindell implicated in a Customs fraud? Or was his connection with the police to be publicly exposed?

Did he, it was retorted, really think that the woman was trying to smuggle jewellery through without her uncle's knowledge? That there was no more in it than that?

He became voluble in denials. He appealed to the sacred skies: did they think him a fool? But he had a doubt which he must test, and, in short, they must await the wire they would get from him. He would have nothing but that.

His prestige, his irritable volubility, his obstinate certainty encountering nothing more resistant than reasoned doubts, had prevailed at last. So it was to be—and so it wasn't at all, for the plan failed. It came to casual disaster at the English Customs, and, at the *Hôtel Splendide*, to a more tragic catastrophe.

The trouble at the Customs arose from the factor which must make all mortal calculation unsure—the physical instability of the human body. There was a Customs officer who was in the confidence of the Yard, and who took instructions from them. He knew what was to be done, and he was not one who would be likely to fail. He was a man in robust health, who would not be expected to fall suddenly ill. Yet fall ill he did, experiencing a sharp bilious attack which he attributed to a sister-in-law's too sanguine belief in the soundness of last Sunday's mutton, which she had curried the night before. But that is a domestic matter we need not probe.

Yet, however unfit he may have felt, he did not go off duty until he had prompted another officer. This was a man who had recently come on the staff, and who appeared to be of more than average alertness, and therefore fit both to take instructions from a senior officer and carry them out intelligently.

He described Kindell to this man, and was explicit upon what should be done. "You needn't be too nosy with him. Just a look-see, and chalk him through."

The man to whom he spoke responded readily. There was no indication that the order would not be exactly obeyed.

But it happened that he had been introduced by the Excise authorities for the especial purpose of detecting corruption, which was suspected among the staff. Neither knew of the secret function the other had. It seemed to him that fortune had opened his way to a discovery from which reward and perhaps promotion would be likely to come.

He watched for Kindell, and made for him with an elbow in a brother officer's side. He took him out of turn, letting other passengers stand impatiently behind their open baggage.

Kindell was not concerned when he saw him approach in this purposeful manner. It was about what he had expected. He opened the suitcase containing the hidden parcel, and another of more orthodox construction, in the expectation that their contents would receive no more than the flick of a carelessly probing hand, while the routine questions were answered in the routine way.

Article by article, his possessions were examined with care. He was closely questioned concerning the origin of those which were least worn. Was it, he wondered with growing impatience, no more than an elaborate pretence? Anyway, he had bought nothing of consequence while in Paris.

But the concealment was not destined to last. The zeal of the baffled officer had now become a conspicuous matter. The baggage of other passengers had been passed, and he operated on an otherwise bare bench. He saw that he must succeed for his own justification, and his conviction that there was something to be discovered remained unshaken. His hands felt along the linings of the emptied case, while he considered the expediency of conducting Kindell to a room where he could be personally searched—and then suddenly he knew. "Do you mind," he asked, with an ominous suavity, "opening the lower compartment of this case?"

Kindell had the wit to look back with blank incomprehension. He said: "I don't know what you mean."

He was answered with a sarcastic: "No? Then I think you soon will."

A little group of interested Customs officials had gathered round them now in the otherwise empty shed. The man measured the outside of the case, and then its interior depth. There was a difference of several inches. He asked: "Don't you see that you'd better open it now?"

Kindell said innocently: "It does look queer. But if there's a pocket, there can't be anything in it. I've never used it. I didn't know it was there," he added in an attempt at natural explanation. "I only bought it quite recently—second-hand."

The man, in his moment of triumph, forgot the restraint of language which official correctitude requires, even in dealing with those who are destined to be heavily fined. He said, "Tell that to the marines." He picked up a knife, with, "Well, if you won't, I must," and slit the lower part of the case. Myra's parcel lay exposed.

"I can only tell you," Kindell said, "that it isn't mine. I'd no idea it was there. I expect you'll have to admit that when you open it. I know you'll find nothing of mine."

It was the best line he could take, while still in ignorance of what its opening would reveal. He knew that something had gone wrong. He knew also that while, if he should be in any serious trouble, there were ways in which he might be protected and helped, his connection with the C.I.D. would not be publicly owned. He might be expected to sacrifice even his personal reputation, even his liberty, to the major interests of the state, and of the criminal investigation in which he was taking a minor

With no thought to spare for an anxious, bewildered Myra, leaning from the window of a first-class carriage as the train began to move slowly along the platform; and still hoping to see him board it at the last second, while trying to persuade herself that he might have escaped her observation, and be already upon the train, he watched the opening of the parcel, and saw a glitter of miscellaneous trinkets scattered upon the bench, among which a shell necklace was the largest, if not the most valuable, article.

With a smile of satisfaction, the officer swept them together again. "You'd better come to the office with me," he said crisply.

"I suppose it's no use telling you again that I've never seen…," Kindell began, in what he now felt to be futile protest, however true.

But he was interrupted by an older officer, who had been watching silently, and now pushed forward to examine the trinkets with experienced eyes. "Talbot," he asked sharply, "what is the charge you propose to make against this gentleman?"

"Well, I should have thought that was clear enough."

"It isn't to me." His fingers moved expertly among the baubles. "It's all rubbish. There's nothing dutiable here."

"Then why on earth did he…?"

"I've told you already that the rubbish is not mine," Kindell interrupted, "and I didn't know it was there. The question is: who's going to pay me for a new case?"

The older officer answered with the diplomatic politeness which the incident had come to require.

"There'll be no difficulty about that, sir, if you send in a claim. We'll find something for you to pack your things in now."

On this pretext, he moved away, drawing with him the officer whose extreme zeal had had so strange a result. As they passed out of Kindell's hearing, his tone changed. "Queer business, Talbot. What made you suspect him?"

"I do still. There's something fishy about it, even if the things aren't worth tuppence."

"So there is. We see some queer things here, but not many queerer than that. What I asked was why you fastened on him the way you did?"

"Because, before Gibbons went off duty, he asked me to pass him without looking too hard, and *that* seemed fishy to me, too."

"Gibbons? You've made a bigger ass of yourself than I supposed. What Gibbons says goes."

"You mean you're all in it with him?"

"In it? In what? Don't be a bigger fool than you've been yet. Gibbons is Scotland Yard."

The jaw of the Excise and Customs detective dropped. He uttered a diminished "Oh."

CHAPTER IX.

MURDER!

KINDELL CONSIDERED what he should do. The train had gone, and Myra doubtless with it. Returning the parcel to her could no longer be important. The question of her arrest, unless upon a charge of complicity too vague for him to define or judge, no longer arose. If at all, it would be at a later date. The event had justified Reynard's doubt. There was probably a telegram of instructions waiting now which would disclose the Frenchman's verification of that which he had deduced before. But the use of that telegram had gone. The incident had taken its own course. His own must be to report to Scotland Yard, and almost certainly be told that his services in this matter were no longer needed. Would that leave him free to tell the Thurlows enough of the truth to put himself right with them? He wished that he could have more confidence in that than he was able to feel. His oath of secrecy was strictly worded, and must be strictly observed. Still, if Blinkwell should be arrested.... But would he? Reynard had been shrewd enough to guess that they were being offered a false scent, but did it follow that he had discovered the real channel by which the smuggling was to be done? He put surmise aside to ask Talbot, who was now offering his assistance to pack the suitcase which had been found to replace the cut one: "Do you know when the next train will leave for Victoria?"

The man was about to reply when his attention was diverted to a uniformed official who held an open telegram in his hand. After a whispered word, he asked, "You are William Kindell?"

"Yes, is that for me?"

"It is a message for you." The man spoke with a gravity which the situation did not seem to require until he added, "You are required to return to Paris at once. Henri Reynard has been murdered."

It was startling, unexpected news, but his profession had accustomed him to take what came without confusion of mind. He asked:

"*Required*? Is it from the Bureau de Sûreté? He frowned at a word which he felt to be ill-chosen, even under such circumstances. His responsibility was not to them.

"No. It is signed Wickham."

Then it was from Scotland Yard. It was an instruction to be obeyed. But he would prefer to know more, if he could. He asked: "When does the boat leave?"

"In about four hours from now."

Then there was plenty of time. Time for a needed meal. Time to get more information as to what he would find in Paris. He went at once to the telephone, got through to London, asked to speak to Mr. Wickham, and heard Superintendent Henderson's voice at the other end of the wire.

He wanted information, and found that he was expected to be able to give it.

"This is a bad business, Kindell. What do you know about it?"

"About what? Reynard being murdered? Nothing at all."

"But I understand you were there at the time?"

"Then you've been told something wrong. Where did it happen?"

"In Thurlow's rooms. The Paris police say it's between you and the ambassador, and naturally you're the one they'd prefer to charge."

"Charge *me*? You know that's absurd. Actually, I knew nothing about it until I heard what you'd wired here."

"But they say you were seen coming out of Thurlow's suite just before the body was found. What can you say to that?"

"I called there before leaving, naturally. They were friends. I can't say what bodies were found after, or where. I know nothing about it. But I'm sure Thurlow wouldn't kill anyone. It's that swine Blinkwell more likely than not."

"I can't say about that. You say Thurlow wouldn't kill anyone. The Paris police don't seem equally sure. They say he's known to be a handy man with a gun."

"And Reynard was shot?"

"I didn't say that. Being quick one way doesn't imply being slow in another. But our Paris friends seem to prefer the idea of you."

"But how can they when they know why I was there? It doesn't make sense. And what motive…?"

"They don't know anything. Reynard did, but he's dead."

"You can let them know."

"But I can't say that we shall. You'll be a lot more likely to get at the truth if no one knows why you were there."

"I don't see that, and besides—"

"But we do. And I don't suppose you'll have any real difficulty. Innocent men aren't guillotined. You'll find our Paris friends will assure you of that. You're best course is to get back as quickly as you can, and let them know you didn't wait to be extradited."

"It sounds pleasant for me."

"Sorry, Kindell, but it's all in the game. And if you *will* go where policemen are being killed, and where you've no business to be—"

"Yes. I see that. Well, I'll get back and find out what I can."

He hung up, conscious rather of a confused excitement of mind than any real fear. It would be absurd to accuse him of such a crime. Yet he saw points which he disliked. It was true that no one but Reynard had known that he was an agent of the English police, true that Reynard's methods were so individual, so secretive, that no one living might know the purpose which had taken him to the *Hôtel Splendide*, or why he should have been in the ambassador's suite. Kindell himself could form no more than a vague conjecture concerning that, though he must accept the fact; Superintendent Henderson was a most unlikely man to be inaccurate, or to extend statements beyond that of which he had been clearly informed. He saw also that, if the murder had been perpetrated in such a manner that suspicion was divided between Thurlow and himself, there might be a very natural official inclination to prefer the less conspicuous *accusé*.

He looked at the clock, and said, "Damn," observing that he still had more than three hours to wait. He had the temperament which prefers to meet trouble quickly, if it cannot be left aside. But that disposition did not prevent him eating a good dinner, or sleeping well on a boat that pitched and rolled as it faced a gusty wind and a choppy sea.

CHAPTER X.

MR. THURLOW IS ANNOYED

CYRIL B. THURLOW, accredited Ambassador Plenipotentiary and Envoy Extraordinary from the United States to the Court of St. James, might or might not be a guilty, but he was certainly a most angry man.

The French have a reputation for being more excitable than the people of his own land, but in this instance the contrast was of a contrary kind. Mr. Thurlow's explosive indignation found itself unable to disturb the calm, or deflect the course, of an investigation which, while treating him with extreme courtesy, was yet of a coldly probing implacability.

Monsieur Samuel's colleagues said that he had no imagination, and that self-confidence born of invincible stupidity had established him in the high position he held—which would, indeed, have been too high to have permitted him to give his time to the details of this investigation, but for the national humiliations or international complications which might arise from any major blunder.

M. Samuel would himself have accepted (with important qualifications) the character which his enemies attributed to him. He would have said that his success was due to the fact that he preferred the obvious and commonplace to the bizarre or recondite explanation of any problem with which he might have to deal. In the result, he had had few spectacular triumphs of which to boast, but his mistakes had been fewer still. So he had come to his present place.

Now he sat opposite Mr. Thurlow, in the lounge of that gentleman's suite, sharing a pleasant fire, and having accepted one of the ambassador's excellent cigars.

"Monsieur—Your Excellency," he said, "that you should be annoyed thus—our regret is extreme. But you will see how we stand. M. Reynard is dead. He was a police officer of France and he has been murdered here. He did not die by his own hand, that is sure.

We do not say it was done by you. We have no cause to suggest! But a motive there must have been. And it is between yourself and Mr. Kindell the deed must lie. You say you are sure it was not he; and beyond that you will tell us nothing at all. It is hard to think that you know as little as that!"

"I tell you I never heard of the man till I saw his dead body lying in the room, on which I rang the hotel office at once. I did not know who he was, nor how he came to be there. Can I be plainer than that? It is for you to explain, and for the hotel management to apologize that they cannot keep my rooms clear of a sight which I was sorry for my daughter to see."

M. Samuel allowed himself to smile slightly at this view of the matter, but continued the conversation without being diverted from the patient, persistent path which he had decided to take.

"You should consider," he said, "that our Bureau can be discreet. It is with us that a confidence may be safely made. There may be questions of mistake, or of self-defence. Even that of justification might be proposed. Our Government would listen to representations made in the right way, coming from one in the position you hold, or from your Government on your behalf, even though M. Reynard's position, and the character that he held—! But you will say nothing at all, and the hours pass! That which may be done now may be impossible on another day."

"I tell you I know nothing at all. Can I add to that?"

"There is this young man you would shield?"

"I would shield no one who shoots men in rooms I have taken at a price which should secure my privacy, unless I know a good reason why, which I certainly don't now."

"Yet Mr. Kindell is a friend?"

"He is slightly related to me."

"If you would tell me why you came to Paris at all?"

"My daughter approves your shops."

M. Samuel shrugged his shoulders slightly. He gave an audible sigh. "And the young man who is slightly related? He would have come for the same cause?"

"I know nothing of that. He did not come with us."

"No, but he was here. I must regret that you will not help me at all. I will see Miss Thurlow now, if you please."

"She can tell you nothing. She was not here at the time."

"That is to be seen."

"Well, I will call her."

"I should prefer to see her alone."

Mr. Thurlow hesitated. Then, with an impatient gesture, he gave way, as he dearly must.

"Very well. You are wasting time. But I waste my own if I tell you that. I will ask Miss Thurlow to see you here."

But as he spoke Irene entered the room. She would have withdrawn when she saw M. Samuel, but her father said: "Irene, you had better answer any questions this gentleman asks. He thinks I have no more sense than to kill strangers who enter my apartment, with a knife that I haven't got."

He walked out as he spoke, leaving M. Samuel to interrogate a girl who now looked at him with wary and hostile eyes.

CHAPTER XI.

IRENE KNOWS NOTHING

IRENE WAS THE first to speak, coming to the point with an abruptness which the Frenchman would not have used. "What is it you want to know?"

"I want you to be kind enough to tell me all you can concerning M. Reynard's death."

"I can soon do that. I know nothing. I went out shopping, and when I came back there was a dead man on the floor."

"At what time was that?"

"Oh, during the afternoon. It was a good while after lunch."

"Can't you be more definite than that?"

"Not unless I guess. When anyone sees a dead man the next thing she does isn't to look at the clock. Not unless it's in books."

"You're not trying to be very helpful."

"I'm not trying either way. I'm trying to make you understand that if you want to find out who did it you're wasting time asking us."

"Who was in the room when you entered?"

"No one except His Excellency. He'd just come in."

"What do you know about Mr. Kindell?"

"He's my cousin."

"Then you probably know the business that brought him over here at the same time as yourselves."

"I might guess and be wrong. It mayn't have been business at all. He's not the sort who'd go about killing strange men in other people's rooms, if you mean that."

"I'm sorry to hear that you have so decided an opinion. Here is a homicide which appears to have been the act of either your father or this young man, and of which we should greatly prefer that His Excellency should be cleared. I hoped that you might be able to give us a pointer in the right direction."

44

"Well, I can't. They're both silly ideas. I've told you my father had only just come into the room."

"How do you know that?"

"He told me himself. I could see how angry he was that the man was there."

"Angry? Surely that is a curious reaction to the discovery of a murdered man? Perhaps his annoyance was that you should see what had occurred?"

"Perhaps it was, more or less. My father is particular about his suite being private and quiet. It's what he's got a right to expect, being who he is. And if he had found it necessary to shoot someone, I don't see how you should interfere. He's an American citizen. You might say he *is* America, having the office he has. Extraterritorial you call it, don't you? Or something like that."

M. Samuel permitted himself a slight smile. "The ambassadorial immunity to which you allude does not extend to a neutral country. His Excellency is not accredited to France. But we are anxious to do what we can to spare him from any annoyance; if—as we are anxious to think—the crime was not his, or even if he could give us any plausible justification for what occurred, our Government might be disposed to receive it in a spirit of tolerance. Our trouble is that neither you nor His Excellency will help us at all."

"But we know nothing about it. What can we say more?"

"You could tell me more of Mr. Kindell than you do. Why did he come up to these rooms at about the time the murder occurred?"

"To say goodbye to me, more likely than not. He was going back to England last night."

"Well, he will be coming back now."

"Then he can tell you himself whatever you want to know."

"Yes. He may see that it will be wise to do that."

M. Samuel's tone indicated that it would be better if others were of the same mind. With a sufficient minimum of courtesy, he got up to go. He thought that after he had talked to Kindell he might persuade the girl to a greater frankness.

He felt that she had already told him more than she was aware, and a theory which would explain much was already taking place in his practical and experienced mind.

CHAPTER XII.

MONSIEUR SAMUEL OVERHEARS

ON ARRIVING in Paris Kindell went straight to the *Hôtel Splendide*, and by so doing obtained about ten minutes' conversation with the ambassador and his daughter before M. Samuel, to whom his movements had been promptly reported, arrived on the scene

He found Mr. Thurlow irritated and Irene worried. They thanked him for the promptness of his return, but in the next moment the ambassador broke out with: "For God's sake Kindell, give us some light, if you can, on this infernal business. The police say you were here in this flat at two-forty-five, and it wasn't three when I came out of my own room and found the man lying here in a filthy mess." He broke off with his eyes on a dark stain which disfigured the cream-and-rose of the Aubusson carpet, large enough to indicate the feature of Reynard's death, which appeared to be most prominent in his orderly mind; and then added, "If you'll tell me on your word of honour that you didn't know the fellow, and had nothing to do with it, of course I'll believe you, but—"

"I couldn't say that exactly." Kindell saw Irene's startled paleness as he made this admission, but her father took it as no more than he expected to hear. He said: "Well, I'm glad you're so frank. Tell us the truth, and we'll do all we can to get you out of the mess."

"I think you misunderstand me. I didn't mean I know anything about the murder. I meant I couldn't say that I'd never met Reynard."

"Then you do know something! You knew the man, and you were here just at the time he was bumped off. If you didn't do it yourself, you must have been within arm's length of the man who did. I tell you, William, as an older man than yourself, and one with more experience of the world, that you're in a tight spot, and your best chance is to hold nothing back, even if it seems to make it blacker for you."

"I can't be franker than I have been already. I had met Reynard, though I don't mean that he was a friend, or I knew him well. But I know nothing about his murder. I didn't meet him yesterday, and I didn't know that he'd come here, till I heard it after I'd landed at Newhaven."

"You'll have to say a lot more if you want to make the cops believe that."

"I'm sorry, but there's really no more to say."

"Can't you understand that we're anxious to help, if you'll only tell us everything while you've got time?"

"I quite understand that. I've shown that I don't want to keep anything back. I needn't have told you that I knew him at all. But I look on you as my friends, and I wasn't going to give you my word of honour to something that wasn't true."

Mr. Thurlow pondered this, gnawing his lips. He asked: "Why do you suppose he came here? To see you?"

"No, I'm sure he didn't."

"How can you possibly be sure unless you know why he did come?"

"I'm sorry, but I can't answer that. I've said too much already. All I can say is that I know nothing about it, and didn't know he'd been shot till—"

"He wasn't shot. He was knifed in the neck."

"And you heard nothing—practically in the next room?"

"There wouldn't be much to hear. If you ever get a knife through your neck from the side like he did, you'll find your larynx isn't in very good vocal order. He must have been struck from behind, a particularly savage blow, and after that—"

"I expect," the voice of M. Samuel interposed, "Mr. Kindell knows as much about that as he can be told." Three pairs of eyes turned towards a door which had been left unlatched, and quietly pushed open without attracting their notice in the tension of their own argument. How much had he heard?

Irene spoke for the first time: "Bill, you've simply got to tell everything now. It's only fair to Father, and it's sure to be best for you."

"I'm sure," M. Samuel said suavely, "that that is just what Mr. Kindell was meaning to do. If you will be so kind as to leave us together—"

"Irene, you'd better come with me," the ambassador said with a decisive sharpness in his voice that his daughter would rarely hear. When they were outside the door he added: "The young man knows a lot more than he's let out yet. When he's finished talking, I reckon that French cop will have been told who the murderer is, or know he can get him without leaving the room."

"I suppose he does," Irene replied in a troubled voice, "but I hope he hasn't got himself into a mess through being confidential to us."

"I wouldn't say that that's quite the word to use," her father replied. He felt too near to being charged with the murder himself to have much patience with the reticence of his young relative, whatever its cause might be. Ambassadors of the United States are not expected to embroil themselves, and perhaps even their Government, with foreign powers by having dead policemen inexplicably littered about their hotel suites. He was not indifferent to any trouble which Kindell—probably by some discreditable folly, if nothing worse—had brought on his own head. But he felt that he should have shown an earlier and completer frankness. He had a duty to his official relative not to involve his name in such a scandal. He must have known, if not of the murder, at least enough to know that he should have stood his ground, and not slipped off to England the way he had. So he said to Irene, who replied, as in explanation, but with the coldness of tone that the name induced, "Miss Blinkwell was going back."

"And you think that was his affair? You're not suggesting that she had something to do with what happened here?"

"You think I don't like her? Perhaps not. But I'm not quite so silly as that. Besides, she left the hotel half an hour earlier."

"I don't care whom you dislike. I only hope you don't—"

"Well, I haven't said that I do."

With this enigmatic exchange, which neither father nor daughter appeared to find any difficulty in comprehending, Mr. Thurlow had turned to pass into his own room, when Kindell's voice was heard, raised to a pitch of angry protest, though the words were inaudible through the thickness of the closed door.

"It sounds," the ambassador added, "as though that young fool's losing his temper. It's a mug's game when you're dealing with foreign cops."

It might have occurred to Irene to retort that her own father's reaction to police enquiries had not been entirely equable, but she only replied: "Men are silly like that. I think I'd better go back and see what the trouble is."

"You'd better stay where you are."

It is improbable that Irene would have accepted this advice had not the voices sunk to a more equable tone. "Well," she said doubtfully, "he ought to be old enough to look after himself. Only, men never are."

CHAPTER XIII.

MR. KINDELL WILL SAY NOTHING

"NOW," M. SAMUEL said, in the assured voice of one who dealt with trivial matters, and has no doubt that his request will be granted as casually as it is made, "perhaps you'll tell me what happened."

"You mean when I called here yesterday afternoon? I just ran up to say goodbye to Miss Thurlow—she's my cousin, you know—and found nobody here, so I didn't stay. I'd only got about three minutes, in any case, before I had to leave for the train."

"Nobody?"

"Mr. Thurlow may have been in his own room. I didn't try to disturb him there."

"And Miss Thurlow may have been in hers?"

"No, I knocked on her door. I'm sure she'd have answered if she'd been there."

"But Mr. Thurlow would doubtless have heard you knock?"

"I don't know. Mr. Thurlow could tell you that best himself."

"So he could. But will he?"

"I've no doubt he would. But I can't see that it matters. It would only show I was here, and I've told you that."

"I must judge of that. We must reconstruct. You saw no one, alive or dead?"

"No, I certainly didn't. A dead body in the middle of a room isn't the sort of thing you overlook or forget."

"But no! We will agree there. And after you left no one came in or out till Miss Thurlow returned a few minutes later, and the dead body was here?"

"How on earth can I say that? I don't know what happened."

"Miss Thurlow came in. We know when you left. You were seen."

"Naturally, I did it openly enough. Probably I was also seen to come up, in which case it will be known that it was a mere moment that I was here."

"It appears that no one saw you come up."

"Or M. Reynard?"

"No, did you come up together?"

"I have answered that already."

"Did you hear anything while you were here? Any sound of voices or other noise? Anything, perhaps, from Mr. Thurlow's room?

"No, nothing at all."

M. Samuel changed the subject abruptly:

"Mr. Kindell, what business had you in Paris?"

"Nothing very definite."

"And the indefinite business was?"

"Nothing to do with murdering M. Reynard, or anyone else."

"Will you answer my question, and leave me to judge of that?"

"I'm afraid I can't add to the answer I have already given."

"Which was no answer at all. Mr. Kindell, do you realize that your attitude must lead, if you are so foolish as to continue it, to your arrest?"

"I don't see what more you can expect me to say. I have told you all I know of the matter, which is practically nothing."

"Pardon me that I cannot agree. You admitted in my hearing that M. Reynard was known to you."

"He must have been known to very many. There is no crime in that."

"But there is a deduction that his call at this hotel was not disconnected with that acquaintance. He knew many who wished that he did not know them. If he called here to detain a gentleman whom he knew to be on the point of leaving Paris—"

"Then why should he have gone to the floor above?"

"He may have been unsure of your room."

"He could have enquired at the desk. Perhaps he did and that would show you that he was not looking for me."

"Of course, we have not overlooked that. He made no such enquiry. But there is a most likely presumption that he saw you on your way to the floor above, and followed you to this apartment."

"And when he got here, I was ready to crawl up behind him and cut his throat with a knife which I keep ready for such occasions? I should call it a grotesque improbability. And all done without a sound that Mr. Thurlow could hear!"

"But it *was* done without any such sound, if Mr. Thurlow is to be believed."

"Then you can conclude that Reynard came here with a definite purpose, and that the man who killed him followed him—not the other way round—with the equally definite purpose of murder, to prevent whatever he was going to do. Find out why Reynard came to this room, and I should say the murderer would be in the bag."

M. Samuel received this advice in a momentary silence, stroking his chin. It was a version of what had occurred which had been present to his own mind, and he saw its probabilities; but he saw also that there were many other possibilities of almost equal plausibility. It was an explanation that might be mere theory, or more probably come from a mind which knew supporting facts which it would not disclose. He was far from sure that he was questioning a guilty man, but he was sure that he could tell him more than he did, and he was resolved both to get at the concealed facts and the motive for their concealment.

"That may be true enough." he answered. "Though it may not be the only explanation of what occurred. But if it were adopted by us, it would do nothing to remove the suspicion which rests upon you. You might yourself have followed M. Reynard, rather than he you."

"And why in heaven's name should I do that? If you will enquire from the English police, you will find that I have no reputation for crawling up hotel stairs to murder people with knives."

"Murder is not a habit, even with most murderers, Mr. Kindell. And a motive is not difficult to imagine. M. Reynard might have been about to disclose to Mr. Thurlow such things as it would have been to your disadvantage for him to know. Perhaps the lady with whom you returned to England could throw some light upon this?"

"I returned to England alone. A lady who was also staying here returned on the same boat. But you can ask her anything that you like, so far as I am concerned. You will waste your time, because she can have nothing to tell you."

As Kindell said these last words, he had a double doubt. He doubted that they went beyond the truth, for it was possible that a close cross-questioning of a frightened Myra might result in disclosures which would put M. Samuel on the right track, if his own theory were right; and he doubted their wisdom, because it was to his advantage that M. Samuel should be so directed, though he could not openly be the one to do it.

But M. Samuel ignored his reply. "She was a lady you knew," he repeated. "You had been out together. You had been entertained in her rooms. Mr. Kindell, I will be plain with you, and you will hear the advice of a man who is much older than you, and more experienced in such matters as this than you can possibly be. I do not know that you killed M. Reynard. But for the fact that someone certainly did, and that it seems to lie between you and another who is an equal improbability, I should call it a most unlikely supposition. And I am impressed by the fact that you came back promptly to face the charge, which was the act of an innocent man, or of a guilty one who is bolder and shrewder than most are. But if you are innocent, you are placing yourself in a great and needless peril; and if you are guilty, you are doing yourself harm rather than good by refusing to be frank with me concerning your relations with the dead man, and other matters which may, or may not, have a bearing upon the crime."

"I am sorry. I believe your advice is sincerely given, and I have no doubt it is good. But I can add nothing to what I have said already. I know nothing of the murder, and I am convinced that Mr. Thurlow is equally ignorant. Till you realize that, you will waste your own time, and allow the murderer more to cover his traces, or get away."

M. Samuel went on patiently, as though he had not heard this reply: "You must remember that you are now subject to French, not to English, law. When we charge a man with murder, we do not allow him to go to sleep in the dock. We think that your rules of evidence are designed to protect guilty rather than innocent men. However that may be, our methods have this result, that an accused person *must* give a coherent and detailed account of his own actions or fall under a suspicion which will almost certainly result in a verdict of guilty, with all its consequences, being recorded against his name.

"In practice, such refusals seldom, if ever, occur. An accused person will always put forward a detailed account of his own movements and relationships to the crime, and it is upon the degree to which they obtain credence, or collapse on close examination, that his fate will largely depend."

"I have no doubt that there is a good deal to be said for your practice," Kindell replied, "and there may be something to be said for ours; but I've got to take things as they are, and nothing alters the fact that I've told you all I can, and the sooner you realize that neither Mr. Thurlow nor I had anything to do with the murder, the sooner you're likely to get on the right track."

M. Samuel rose. He said: "Mr. Kindell, you must not think me rude if I quote a proverb of your own country. Experience keeps a dear school—"

"—but fools will learn in no other. You need not hesitate to complete it. Will you think me even ruder than you if I add that there are some whom even that school seems unable to teach? Surely your experience should enable you to distinguish between innocent and guilty men."

M. Samuel showed no sign of offence at the implications of this reply. He said: "You will give me your word, Mr. Kindell, that you will remain here?"

"I did not come back for the purpose of running away. I shall not leave the hotel without letting you know."

"I accept your word." M. Samuel bowed and left.

CHAPTER XIV.

MR. KINDELL AS LIVE BAIT

AS M. SAMUEL left, Mr. Thurlow and Irene returned to the room.

"I hope," the ambassador said, "that you have been able to give the police the information which they require."

His tone was that of one who is unsure whether he has cause for quarrel or complaint, or of how serious it may be; and there was no satisfaction to be found in Kindell's reply: "I told him what I told you, that I know nothing about it at all."

"But after he had heard you say that you knew the dead man, he would want something better than that."

"Then it's something that he can't get."

"If he should arrest you, you'll find that that will be a very dangerous attitude to adopt."

"I'll worry about that if he tries it on."

"Will," Irene interposed, looking at him with troubled eyes, "I don't know why you're making such a mystery of it, but if you really weren't here when it happened, is it quite fair to Father—or me? It's plain to everyone that you know something you're holding back, and, if you'd be frank about it, whatever else it did, it couldn't help getting Father out of the mess."

"You're quite sure that that would be the result?"

"It seems sense to me."

"Well, I'm sorry I can't say more. The whole trouble is that M. Samuel heard me say more than I ought to have done to you."

"I don't see that you did. You said next to nothing. You only said that you knew M. Reynard. There's no crime in that."

"That is precisely the point of view which I recommended to M. Samuel's consideration."

"Well, it's sense. It isn't what you said but what you won't say that's making trouble."

"Rene," her father interposed, "it's no use arguing that Bill hasn't said anything. He's said a mouthful. I don't know why he won't trust us by spitting the whole tale out, but if he thinks it's better to keep it back, we're not going to press him to tell it because it might be helpful to us. No, sir! If that's how you feel, we're not asking you to open anything up. Not for our sakes, that is. But if you did it for your own, you might be a wiser man than you are."

In the voice with which this was said, even more than the words themselves, there was an implication of offence, if not of distrust, which Kindell could not fail to hear. He looked at Irene, and it was plain that she shared her father's feelings.

They thought that he was leaving the ambassador under a cloud of unjust suspicion, which might be lightened, if not removed, by a frank statement of what he knew of the dead man. It was a natural presumption, for that he should have known him and yet had no connection with his presence there, and that such knowledge was of a nature he could not disclose either to his own friends or to those who were investigating the crime, were propositions of exceptional improbability. And if they should seek in their own minds to excuse his reticence?—the more substantial the excuse, the more seriously must they suppose him to be involved in some illicit activity, if not actually in the crime itself. Yet what more could he say?

"Well, if you won't trust me...," he began.

Irene interrupted acutely. "You don't give us a chance. You're not trusting us."

"Yes," he said, "I can see how it looks to you."

He went back to his room, which was not the one he had had before, but one next to that which Professor Blinkwell still occupied, which he had given notice that he would be vacating on the following day, when he would return to England.

Kindell did not interpret the undertaking he had given to M. Samuel as a pledge that he would not leave the precincts of the hotel, but he had no inclination to go out into the crowded life of the Paris streets. He paced the room restlessly, debating what he could do in the enigmatic position in which he stood, either to regain Irene's confidence or to solve the mystery of Reynard's murder.

Finding no satisfaction in this solitude, and yet reluctant to put such thoughts aside, he ordered dinner to be served in his own room, and supposed, when he gave casual assent to a discreet knock, that the waiter was at the door. But it was M. Samuel who entered.

"You will spare me a few moments?" The tone was friendlier than he had expected to hear, but he did not feel an inclination for further verbal fencing with the self-confident detective. If he meant to arrest him, well, there was no more to be said! If not, well, that was still the same. He said curtly, "I have just ordered dinner."

M. Samuel showed no offence. "We have examined M. Reynard's papers," he said.

"Naturally."

Kindell's interest was aroused now, but he was still warily reticent.

"We have also had a further conversation with London. We have learnt much."

"Perhaps you will join me at dinner?"

"I thank you, no, I have dined. But I will sit with you, and take a glass of wine, if you will."

"As you please. Perhaps you will order what you prefer."

The waiter, as he spoke, was already in the room. M. Samuel gave his order. As the man retired, the detective asked: "Are you undisturbed here? Do you hear sounds at times from adjoining rooms?"

"No, nothing. I should say these are solid walls. But I have not had this room previously."

"Yet I think we may feel secure."

Having said this, M. Samuel became silent. The waiter came again, and withdrew, and still he gave Kindell the opportunity to be the first to speak, as at last he did.

"I suppose you are satisfied that I am not a murderer now?"

It was a question which told nothing, but invited a reply which might tell much.

"Personally, yes. Officially—that is another matter."

"That is difficult to understand. Whatever more you know now must have been officially learned."

"Yet so it is."

The reply irritated Kindell. Why could not the man talk in a plain way? He said: "Well, personally's enough for me. If you'll be good enough to tell Mr. Thurlow that you're personally sure that I didn't kill Reynard, I won't ask anything more."

M. Samuel neither assented nor showed any resentment at the tone of this reply. He said: "I have a message for you from Mr. Wickham. He wishes you to co-operate with us—to do anything that we may require."

"Then you know perfectly well—"

"I am coming to that. Mr. Wickham said that you could telephone him for confirmation of our instructions, if you should feel it necessary to do so. But he thought it would be wiser not to communicate with him in any way."

"Perhaps I can judge better if I hear from you what those instructions are."

"We wish you to let Professor Blinkwell know that you are suspected of Reynard's murder."

"Suspected by you?"

"Yes."

"What is the object of that? He will not easily believe. He must have concluded already that I am an agent of the police."

"Must he? I am less than sure. Or, if he did, may he not be disposed to change his opinion now? The way you were treated in the Customs may support his doubt."

"He may not even have heard of that."

"Then you must tell him."

"Which would be betraying his daughter's confidence, for which I see no plausible reason."

"Then you must act as seems best to you. I should think you could do it in a most natural way. But we do not wish to dictate the details of what you do. It is as a man of ability that you are recommended to us. We want you to act precisely as one would do who had had your experiences, and had had no connection with us. And we shall act to you in the same way."

"Not precisely, I hope? I'm not still under danger of arrest?"

"I cannot say that, but if you should be arrested, I need not say that you will disclose nothing. We must subordinate all to the discovery of the murderer, and to bring the work he was doing to a success which M. Reynard would have approved."

"You will say sufficient to Mr. Thurlow and his daughter to clear me with them?"

"That is of such importance to you? I regret that it is a promise I cannot give. Is it not Miss Blinkwell whose good opinion you are most anxious to have?"

"Damn Miss Blinkwell. Yes, I see what you mean. I must leave it to you. We must hope it will not be long."

M. Samuel, having finished his wine, got up to go. "So we may," he agreed. "Which may rest with you. At present you are experiencing much questioning from the police. There should be no secret of that."

CHAPTER XV.

AN EFFORT IN MENDACITY

BEING LEFT ALONE, Kindell faced the fact that he was cast for a part which he did not like.

There was the probability, if no more, that he was to be arrested for the murder of Reynard, and, for a time at least, he must allow it to appear that he could not clear himself of the charge. He was to allow his friends to convict him, in their own minds, of folly, if not of guilt, and to conclude either that he distrusted the quality of their friendship or had acted in a manner which he was ashamed to reveal.

And, as an immediate requirement, he was to act a part which would be difficult to assume, and with a most dubious possibility of any credit or success resulting. He had to act as would be natural to one in his position who had been inexplicably and (as it would seem) pointlessly tricked by Professor Blinkwell's niece, and who was under suspicion of having committed an atrocious crime.

What would an innocent young man, new to such experiences, naturally do? He would look round for friends. He would seek their confidence and support. On both the strange experiences of the last twenty-four hours, it was to the Professor that it would be natural for him to go. So he must, and at once, or his omission to do so would have a significance which the Professor would be quick to see.

But Professor Blinkwell was a most astute, and would surely be, a suspicious man. He might *know* that he was dealing with a police agent, in which case it would be an impossible enterprise. He certainly suspected it; and that suspicion would be difficult to remove.

Well, there would be no gain in delay. He was an innocent, puzzled, and angry man, with no clue to the meaning of the events in which he was involved! Resolving to sustain this mood, to the exclusion of truth even in his own thoughts, he left his room and knocked on the Professor's door.

Professor Blinkwell received him with his usual suavity, but with some distance of manner.

"You have come back," he said, "more quickly than you had planned when you left."

The tone was noncommittal, as that of one who had heard dubious tales, but would not be hasty to judge.

"Yes," Kindell replied, "it's this ghastly murder upstairs. They'd make out I'd got something to do with it, if they could. But I've no doubt you've heard about that?"

"I have heard," the Professor replied, "that a French policeman was found dead, and presumably not by his own hand, in the room of a United States ambassador upstairs, but I should not have connected it with you, which has an improbable sound, even if you had not (as I suppose) already left the hotel when the unfortunate incident occurred. But I will not conceal from you that there was conversation in the lounge in the last hour which has prepared me for what you say."

"Well, that's how it is, and I thought you might be able to advise me what best to do."

"If," the Professor said, with a deliberation which might be taken to imply that, though by no means sure where the truth might lie, he was keeping a scrupulously open mind, "you had nothing whatever to do with it, I should say you could not do better than to go on doing nothing at all. Unless the police here have conclusive evidence of a kind which is hardly possible under such circumstances, I should say that they would be reluctant to drag you in. It has," the Professor concluded, with a slight smile, "an aspect of involving three nations instead of two."

"I'm sorry that M. Samuel does not appear to regard it in that way. He seems to think that to fasten it on to me is the best conclusion he can desire."

"And you really know nothing about it?"

"Nothing at all."

"You observed nothing to rouse your suspicions, or which would be helpful to the police?"

"No, nothing at all."

"Well, you had better tell me just what happened as far as you are concerned. If I can help you by advice or in other ways, you can be sure that it will be done. I should have thought the police would have had the sense to see that you are not the sort to be concerned in such an affair. Had you any acquaintance with M. Reynard?"

The question was asked casually, and the Professor's eyes expressed nothing but friendly enquiry and concern, but it was well for

Kindell that he had foreseen its probability, and prepared himself for an instant denial.

"No," he said readily. "I've only been in Paris once or twice in my life, and then only for weekends. It isn't reasonable to suppose that I should be personally acquainted with the police here, let alone want to murder them. It seems too absurd to take seriously."

"Yes, it is a strong point," the Professor agreed, but in a tone of gravity which did not diminish as he went on, "but it is always difficult to prove a negative. And the police require you to satisfy them of your innocence in this country, rather than that they should be able to prove your guilt. Still, if they can suggest no motive, I should say that you have little to fear. Some temporary inconvenience, perhaps. And some expense. You will be able to deal with that? You should have a good lawyer for your defence. Perhaps you will let me help? As a friend of Myra's—and, talking of her, does she know of this trouble? Was she with you when it was brought to your knowledge?"

"No, she had gone on to the train."

Kindell paused in a way which suggested that there was something more which might be said, but upon which he hesitated. It seemed to him a natural attitude to adopt, for, however puzzling the event might have been to one in the state of ignorant subservience to Myra's wishes which had been his assumed part, the bewildering sequel had been hardly such as would have led him to betray the transaction to the uncle whom (she had said) it had been her first object to mislead.

The Professor looked what may have been genuine surprise. "She must," he said "have been in a more independent and energetic mood than is usual with her when she has a companion on whom to lean."

Kindell saw the use of a limited frankness which would tell the Professor that which he would yet appear to be scrupulous to conceal.

"There was," he said hesitantly, "a little difficulty with the Customs. The fact was that they discovered a false bottom in a suitcase which I had bought second-hand here. It contained a parcel of jewellery of which I had not, of course, been aware, about which they were naturally difficult to convince."

"It will mean some further trouble for you?"

"No, the articles were, fortunately, mere trinkets. Of no value at all."

"It was a fortunate end to what must have been an unpleasant episode."

"Yes, but it had caused a good deal of delay, and Myra had gone on to the train."

"Where she would have expected you to join her?"

"Yes, she would."

"And she must still be ignorant of all that has transpired subsequently?"

"Yes. As I got free from the Customs, I had a police message saying that a murder had been committed on which they required to interview me, and requesting my immediate return to Paris."

"Which you were under no compulsion to obey?"

"Obviously not, but it would have been foolish to refuse."

"Perhaps it would. As you knew nothing about it, it must have been a most surprising message?"

"I was amazed."

"Well, as you say you know nothing about it, I do not see what you can do better than to await the next move by the police. But perhaps you would prefer to be more actively occupied? Perhaps you are disposed to make your own enquiries, with a view to discovering the perpetrator of the crime?"

"It doesn't sound a very attractive proposition. As a stranger in Paris, what possible chance should I have, if the police have no success?"

"I have no doubt you are right," the Professor agreed readily. "But it is not everyone who will take so reasonable a view. The successful amateur detective is a creation of popular fiction. In reality I should say he is an impossible character. Well, let me know of whatever development there may be, and you can depend upon any help I can give, both for Myra's sake and your own."

With these words they parted. Kindell went back to his own room with no certainty that he had deceived a man whom he recognized as a master of successful duplicity; but he had some hope, mainly based upon the introduction of Myra's name, and the Professor's apparent wish to emphasize the acquaintance with his niece, even beyond fact.

Actually, Professor Blinkwell was left with a disturbing doubt. He had had a confident belief that Kindell was a police agent when he had used Myra to plant that parcel of worthless jewellery upon him. He had planned to lead the police on that false scent while he had been disposing of the illicit parcel in another way. He had met him now with the same assumption in his mind. He had thought, with that unsuspected knowledge at the back of his mind, that he might learn much, and could rely upon his own verbal adroitness to give nothing away.

But now he was left in doubt. Kindell's alloy of frankness and reticence in regard to the parcel with which Myra had entrusted him had been skilfully contrived, but it might have been insufficient in itself to shake an opinion based upon information from a source which the Professor had found reliable on previous occasions. But there was also the incident at the Customs, which was very difficult to reconcile with the supposition that the parcel was being conveyed with the knowledge and approval of the police.

As he pondered this part of the problem, he experienced a degree of irritation he rarely felt. He saw that, if Kindell were not connected with the police, he had busied himself in a particularly useless and foolish manner. That was cause for irritation enough, for he was of a sensitive vanity. But to be unsure—that was more irritating still.

CHAPTER XVI.

IRENE RESOLVES TO TRY

"YOU MEAN," MR. THURLOW asked, that I am not free to leave?"

M. Samuel was ceremoniously polite. "But not at all! It is not *required*. It will be a favour to us. It is so I ask, and that you will take it no other way."

"I take it," the ambassador replied, "in the only way that I can. And I will tell you this: it is a request which I would refuse, if I were of a disposition to go. I would challenge you to prevent me, if your Government were of no better discretion than that. I can tell you that I have discussed the matter with Mr. Rolls"—Rolls was the U.S. Ambassador accredited to the French Republic—"and he is of the same mind. It is not suspicion, it is apology which is due to me. It was an intrusion upon the amenities of my visit here, such as the English police would not allow to occur—let alone providing an exhibit from their own ranks, such as you were regrettably unable to prevent. But I will tell you this. I intend that this affair shall be cleared up, and I will put the best detectives from my own country upon it, at whatever cost to myself, if that is more than you are able to do. For the present, I shall remain here, unless my official duties shall require my return, in which event I shall go at once, relying upon the passport I hold, and with no reference to you."

M. Samuel rose stiffly. "If you are staying, it is all that I have asked. And you may have opportunity to see that our police are no less efficient than those of your own land."

Mr. Thurlow said no more. He was an angry man. He had read what the continental edition of the *New York Herald* had to say on the event, and he did not like it; for, though it might have been worse, there had been an absence of the reticence which the French police had required of their own press; and he had already had some cabled summaries of what was being published in his own country, which he liked even less. He did not forget that the party to whom he owed his appointment was no longer in the ascendancy either in Congress or at the White House. Was his career to be wrecked by this incident, for which he had no responsibility at all and which it would have been impossible to foresee? It was a maddening possibility. And that young fool on the floor below—if he could be induced to speak!

"Irene," he exclaimed abruptly, "can't you make him see sense?"

Irene understood readily, and her hesitation did not arise from any lack of appreciation of her father's position. She said, "You think it's that serious? I don't mind trying."

"I wish you would. If he'll only be frank with us, you can tell him it shan't go further without his consent."

"Well, I'll try."

"And I'll have a cable put through to Washington. I'd like to give Hammond a tip on how to deal with this."

The announcement of this decision gave Irene an increased realization of the gravity with which her father regarded the incident, and increased her determination to persuade her cousin to a franker attitude.

But her efforts to find him were not immediately successful. He was not in his room, and when he was located, it was in the dining room, where she was indisposed to intrude upon him.

Before she could telephone him in the privacy of his own room, her father had been on the Washington line, and though it was a conversation she did not hear, she could judge something of with whom, and what its purport had been, when he said to her: "We're going back to London at once—by the night boat. I don't know what I'm suffering from, unless its senile decay, but I ought to have said that at once, when M. Samuel had the damned insolence to hint that I'd better stay."

"Then I'd better begin packing now. Shall we go by air?"

"No, but we'll take the next boat, and I'll let Samuel know what I intend. That'll give him a few hours to think things over before he decides whether to do anything that'll put him in the ranks of the unemployed—and perhaps me as well, which would matter more."

"Yes, I see." So, being an intelligent girl, she more or less did. Washington did not wish to have an ambassador to England who was detained by the French police; or, at least, it wished to know with certainty whether that was the position with which it would have to deal. Her father had been told to call for the cards to be turned up, so that they would know where they were.

Well, there might be all the more reason for plain talking to William now!

So she went to the phone again, and heard Kindell say, but with a reserve in his voice which, faint though it was, she did not fail to detect and resent:

"Yes, of course. Glad to. Shall I come up now?"

"No, I'll come down to you."

There was a moment's pause before he answered, "Very well, if you'd rather," the hesitation being more evident than before. It gave Irene a momentary fear that he had considered that there was some breach of propriety in her proposal to visit him in his own room. Could there be? Between cousins? In the afternoon? By English standards, if not by hers? She put the foolish idea aside. Let him think what he would—he would quickly learn that there was no levity in her mind.

But when she reached his room she could not tell herself that there was any lack of cordiality in his reception, and if it failed something in the spontaneity of his usual manner—well, perhaps it was natural! Particularly if he had guessed the purpose for which she came.

"Anything fresh?" he asked, as he drew forward his most comfortable chair.

"Yes, I should say there is! That beast Samuel has had what Father calls the damned insolence to hint that we'd better stay where we are, and Washington's told us to start back to London at once, and see whether they've got the nerve to stop us."

"I don't think they'll do that."

"I wish for Father's sake that I were equally sure. I don't mean that I'm afraid of any serious trouble for him over the murder. That's ridiculous. But it's the fact of one in his official position getting mixed up in such an affair."

"I don't see that. If he had no part in it—about which I'm as sure as you—it would be absurd to blame him for something he couldn't reasonably have been expected to foresee or prevent."

"Of course it would. But politics aren't reasonable. And it's different with us from what it is in England. Our diplomatic appointments are matters of party politics, and are liable to be attacked in ways that you wouldn't know. If a Republican gets mixed up in an unpleasant affair, the Democrats think it's only playing the game to make it look as bad as they can. And if they can make it ugly enough for the Republican bosses to think that they'd get on better without the man the talk's about, it doesn't matter who he is, or whether he's right or wrong. They'll throw him overboard.

"In your country, I've heard that a scandal's sometimes hushed up by the Press to save a good man from getting sacked. But that wouldn't be possible in America. If we go wrong, it's the opposite way. And that," she concluded, with an earnest pleading in her voice which was not pleasant for Kindell to hear, "is why we feel we're in rather a jam, and why I'm going to ask you to be franker with us than you've been yet."

"You think I know something about it I haven't said?"

"I'm sure you do."

"And you think it would help your father if I said it?"

"Yes, it's common sense. Anything that gets nearer to what *did* happen must be helpful to him."

Kindell rose, and paced the room restlessly. He had found himself incapable of the ready unconvincing lie which M. Samuel might have said that the position clearly required, and he saw that his delay in replying was an admission of knowing more than he was willing to say.

"You know, Irene," he began at length, "I don't want to keep anything back from you—"

"Then we both feel the same. I'll promise we won't let it go further without your consent."

It appeared certain to Kindell that the French police would not venture—probably would not even wish—to detain the ambassador, when they knew that he intended to defy their request for him to remain in Paris. Is it wrong to make a conditional promise which you would not keep, if you are certain that the condition will not arise? It is a point of casuistry to which he had no time to give the full consideration which its subtlety surely requires. He scrambled onto the precarious raft it offered, when he said: "I can't say more than this. If your father should be detained by the police here—I don't think he will be—I'll tell you everything that I know or guess about the whole affair."

"I don't think I'm going to say thank you for that. It would be offering help when it would be too late to be any good."

"I suppose you see that I'm under suspicion as well as Mr. Thurlow? And most people would say that I'm in more danger. The police here haven't any reason to be afraid of arresting me."

"That's just an extra reason why you shouldn't keep anything back from us. We're not keeping anything from you. Can't you treat us as friends? Or are the Blinkwells the only people you feel able to trust?"

Irene had a moment of immediate regret at this last question which was impulsively put. But next minute she was less sure that she had been wrong, as he replied, "I never said that I trusted them," and she had a sound instinct that the suggestion had caused embarrassment rather than indignation or surprise.

"No," she said, rising in a resentment which she felt to be the last card that she had to play, "you know best about that. But it's evident that you don't trust us. I'd always hoped that when I came to Europe, I should meet relatives it would be a pleasure to know. But we all make mistakes sometimes."

She had certainly made him look unhappy now. But his only reply was: "I'm very sorry you feel like that. How do you propose to get back to England?"

"We're going on the night boat. Almost at once."

"I think I'll do the same, or at least try to. I shall have to let Samuel know. He won't arrest both of us, and, if he doesn't let us both go, he's more likely to choose me. When we meet in London, I may be able to say more than I can now."

If he had thought that this suggestion of drawing the lightning to his own head would placate her, he quickly learnt his mistake as she answered: "If we happen to meet, of course I'll listen to anything that you have to say. But Father might think that he'd rather not have any more murders you can't explain."

It was again more than she had meant to say, and was unlike herself in the mixture of exaggeration and injustice which it contained, but she was wounded by his lack of confidence in herself, troubled by her father's position, and humiliated by the necessity of going back to tell him that she had so completely failed.

She left abruptly without either a formal leave-taking such as acquaintance requires, or an affectionate one such as friendship prefers, and where she told her father the substance of what had passed, he said easily: "Well, honey, I reckon it's best that way. I figure he's in it up to the neck, and we might have only dirtied our hands trying to pull him out of the mud. He's a young fool, all the same. And if he's chumming up to that half-bred Jewess, I'd say he's just running after one of his own kind."

Meanwhile, Kindell was on the telephone with the Bureau de Sûreté, the defiant tone of his conversation being intended rather for the ears of the operator at the hotel switchboard (whom he rightly supposed to be an interested auditor) than for those of the intelligent policeman to whom he spoke.

Ten minutes later there were few of the hotel staff who did not know (under pledge of secrecy from one whisperer to another) that Mr. Kindell, already vaguely understood to be involved in the mystery of the Reynard murder, had been told that he could not leave

Paris, and had expressed his determination to do so, even after he had been warned that such an attempt must lead to his immediate detention.

There was consequently little surprise when two detectives arrived, and, after a short interview in the room of the suspect, led him downstairs in evident arrest, and with an aspect of dejection such as the event would be likely to cause, to be removed in a waiting car.

His short interval of freedom had been mainly spent in Professor's Blinkwell room, whose sympathy had been readily given, and who had advised him, with as much emphasis as his habitual suavity of manner allowed, to remain obstinately silent under whatever pressure from the police. "I should assert and insist upon the principles of our traditional English justice," he had said, "against whatever pressure you may encounter. You will find it your best protection against the methods they will employ, being both as innocent and as ignorant, as you say, and as I do not hesitate to believe. And this attitude will be likely to avail you as it would not one of their own countrymen. I would myself come to court to give you any support that would be in my power, but I am unfortunately obliged to return to England by the night boat, there being a board meeting in London I must not fail to attend."

After Kindell left him, he continued to sit in motionless thought, as he faced one of the most perilous hours that his life of successful criminality had so far known.

Only once before had he become so closely involved in the drug-smuggling activities which he largely controlled; never had he faced crisis with such a feeling of being bankrupt of expedient or resource. Since his last conversation with Kindell, he was increasingly disposed to think that he had been misinformed concerning his connection with the police. If that were so, it reduced, to some extent, the presence of surrounding danger. But what a fool it made of himself! How abortively the precious hours had been lost! How silly that business of Myra and the smuggled parcel had been. He picked up the service telephone, and said that he would have some refreshment served at once in his own room. Yes, at once. He was leaving by the boat train. Gustav knew what he liked. Perhaps he could bring it up?

It was within ten minutes that his favourite waiter appeared, with a meal which might be all he desired, but to which he gave no immediate attention; and the conversation which followed was not such as is usual between waiter and guest.

"They've just arrested Monsieur Kindell," the man said, as he closed the door, after wheeling the dumb-waiter into the room.

"But," the Professor asked, "did it look like the real thing?"

"He looked sick enough. But I wouldn't say that I'm sure yet."

"Well, we've got to make up our minds. It seems most probable that Prestwick gave us a bad tip."

"He's never done that before."

"But he seems to have done it now. Anyhow, Kindell's out of the way, and that's given us a chance that we mustn't miss."

For whatever degree of error the Professor might blame himself in the events of the last week, he was instant now to perceive the possibility which was opened by Kindell's arrest; and, as he spoke, he had abandoned the hazardous plan which he had been driven to entertain and had substituted another, not only such as would give a greater probability of success, but which shifted the penalties of failure from his own shoulders, as he had always previously contrived.

"What," he asked, "has been done with Kindell's luggage?"

"It was sealed by the police. The room also is locked and sealed."

"But Kindell, fearing arrest, as the Thurlows will know he did, might have placed a valise in your hands?"

"Yes," Gustav agreed. "So he might." But his tone was reluctant, and he looked at Professor Blinkwell with apprehension, for he was as cautious by temperament as the Professor himself, which may be the explanation of why he was, perhaps, the only active member of the whole drug-trafficking gang of whom the police had no suspicion at all.

"So," Professor Blinkwell went on smoothly, "we will suppose that he did. What would be his natural course? He would entrust it to you to hand to Miss Thurlow or to her father, to take charge of it for him, which they would scarcely refuse."

Gustav looked doubtful now, as well as unwilling. "Do you think not?"

"Yes, he is their cousin. But if I should be wrong you will be better off than you are now."

"That is hard to see."

"It is plain enough. You will have an explanation of how it comes to be in your hands, which, unless you have asked the Thurlows to take it, you could not use. It would be calling yourself a thief to say that he had put it in your charge for such a purpose, and you had not taken it to them."

"But it is not in my hands. It is where, if it should be found, it could not be connected with me."

"Perhaps not. But would you not become suspect to the police, together with all who are employed here? They would search the records of all. They would watch you by night and day. Would you like that?

"But if you place it in Thurlow's hands you are clear at once. He may pass it to England without suspicion being aroused, and we shall have foiled the police again, as we have done so often before. Or, if it be disclosed, you have a complete reply. You had it from Kindell, and were an innocent messenger, as any other of the staff here might have been."

"The police would not look at it in that way. Even if they should think I had known nothing of its contents, I should be held to have conspired to conceal the property of a criminal under arrest."

The Professor showed some irritation at this point, as he was practised to do at the right time.

"Gustav," he said, "I have known you for ten years, and it is the first time that I have been tempted to call you a fool. Would Kindell have been arrested when he gave the valise to you? Were his effects sealed by the police then?

"I am not showing you a way in, but a way out. Do you suppose that I place no value upon you as one whom the police do not suspect?

"But I will go further. If the Thurlows refuse the case (which I do not expect), you can ask their advice, and if they say take it to the police, as they would then be most likely to do, you shall do that.

"That will be a loss of £6,000, which I shall not like; but it will convince the police that you are an innocent man, and that it is Kindell who smuggles drugs."

"That is, if he is not their agent?"

"Even then they may be unsure. Have you heard our proverb of those who run with both hare and hounds? It would explain to them why they have been baffled so long. And it would not be the Sûreté here, but Scotland Yard which would have been so befooled. They would be no less disposed to believe it for that. But you lose time, and you may be too late for the best chance we shall have." Gustav went at that, half-convinced, and wholly subdued by the stronger will, and Professor Blinkwell finished his meal with a more peaceful mind than he had had for the last week. Danger had been nearer to him than he would usually allow it to come, but now he saw it moving farther away.

He regained the cool self-confidence also, on which he had learnt to rely, but which had been shaken by the doubt of whether he had acted foolishly in regard to the way in which Myra had been employed. But if he had been misled by a subordinate's error, he had not failed to take swift advantage of the opportunity offered by Kindell's arrest, which many might have failed to see.

His only doubt was whether he might not have done better still to instruct Gustav to take the valise straight to the police, with the tale that Kindell had instructed him to give it to Thurlow but that he had feared lest he should be doing something of which the law might not approve. It would certainly cause confusion in the counsels of those who were so uncomfortably close upon him, being of the subtlety with which he had outwitted them often before, but still it would be a loss of £6,000—of drugs for which British addicts were hungry now. He might do much better than that.

CHAPTER XVII.

IRENE CAN CHANGE HER MIND

GUSTAV KNOCKED AT the door of the Thurlows' flat, and found that the ambassador was alone. "Can I speak to Miss Thurlow?" he asked, having decided that he would do better with her. Irene was packing in her own room.

Her father said curtly: "She is busy now. What do you want?"

Gustav saw that it would be impolitic to appear unwilling to give a frank answer. He said: "It is a message from Mr. Kindell. He asked if you would be kind enough to convey this valise to London on his behalf, if he should be detained here."

"Detained by the police?"

"That was how I understood it to be."

"Why did he not come himself?"

"How can he come, he being under arrest?"

That was news to Mr. Thurlow. Irene and he, having been occupied in packing in their own rooms, may have been the only people in the hotel who were not already aware that Kindell had been removed in the escort of the police.

"Has he been arrested? Is he still in the hotel?"

"He was taken away about an hour ago."

As Gustav answered, he observed that Irene had entered the room from its opposite door. Seeing him, and hearing what was I said, she stood still.

Her father's questions continued sharply. "Then do the police know of this? Did you bring it with their consent?"

"He gave it to my charge before they had arrived."

"Then you must tell him that it is a matter with which I can have nothing to do."

"How can I do that, now that he is gone? It is very awkward for me."

"Then you should hand it to the police."

"Mr. Kindell said that it was so small a thing that he was sure mademoiselle would not refuse."

This was Gustav's last effort, for the programme of surrendering it to the police was one which even with Professor Blinkwell's permission, he was reluctant to adopt, and it had an immediate effect.

Irene came forward, so that her father became aware of her presence. She asked, "Did you bring a message to me?"

"It was you whom I was instructed to see."

"And Mr. Kindell really has been arrested?"

"Yes. He has been removed by the police."

"Then you can leave the valise here."

"Irene," her father said sharply, "I forbid you to have anything to do with that young man's baggage."

But Gustav had laid the valise down already, and left the room. He thought that the probability that the valise would be delivered in London had become very great.

So it had. Irene had had a miserable hour, being unsure of several things she was anxious to know, but having become aware of one—that she had been both unkind and unfair. Being miserable, she was in a mood to quarrel with someone, and here was an opportunity put into her hand, and her father would suit her requirements better than a stranger could have been expected to do.

"He's our cousin," she said. "We're surely not going to let him down over a small thing like that."

"It mayn't be a small thing at all. I don't trust him: he wouldn't trust us, and he can't expect that we should."

"Isn't he trusting us now? You talk as though that may be where he's going wrong."

"He's beginning a bit late."

"Haven't you thought that we may have got him all wrong? He's in some kind of a mess over this murder. That's plain enough. But he didn't do it. Nobody'd make me believe that. And if he wouldn't say more to us, it may have been because he didn't want to get us in with him. And if that's how it is, he wouldn't have asked us to do this if it would mean any real risk for you."

"It's no use saying that, Rene. He thought he would be arrested, and he's trying to get rid of something he doesn't want the police to see."

"Of course he is. But that doesn't mean it's anything wrong. If I were going to be arrested, I've got lots of things I shouldn't want to be pawed over by them Or talked over in court more likely than not. And you'd feel just the same. How can you think of playing that man Samuel's game after his rudeness to you! I should say we'd be the two meanest skunks—"

Irene left the sentence unfinished, for she saw, with experienced eyes, that she was chastising a beaten man.

"Well," her father said wearily, "if you look at it like that! But I don't want to know anything about it, whatever happens."

"Well, why should you? The message was meant for me."

Irene had now picked up the valise, and concealed her surprise at its weight. Was it solid gold? Well, it was no business of hers! She had chosen her part, and felt that her honour and her cousin's forgiveness were alike staked upon getting it safely to the address which was—curiously enough, as she was aware, but she was not in the mood for critical comment—written upon a tie-on label in an obviously foreign hand. And there was no name! But might that not be a reasonable precaution? Obviously, he would give them the ad- dress to which he would wish it to be forwarded after its arrival in England. It might be considered equally obvious that he would not put his own name on an article of luggage which was to be carried by them. That would be to give its secret away even before it had left the hotel, it being of a weight which required that it should be left to the porter's hands.

Thinking this, and with a sense of comradeship in outwitting the police which was much more pleasant to feel than the previous an- ger, Irene took off the label, put it into an inner pocket of her hand- bag, and substituted another on which she wrote, not her own name, but that of her father, with full assertion of his ambassadorial office, and an injunction that it was to be treated with special care.

Having completed this lawless work, she continued her own packing with a happier mind than she had had previously, in spite of some natural anxiety as to her cousin's position. She thought with satisfaction that he had had sense enough to know who his real friends were. Had he preferred to trust the uncle of that unwieldy Jewess, it would have been very hard to forgive!

CHAPTER XVIII.

IN WHICH EVERYONE FEELS RELIEF

BOTH PROFESSOR BLINKWELL and the Thurlows chose to return to England by the Calais-Dover route, which was more convenient for night travelling, owing to the ferry service which had recently been instituted. They could go to bed on the train in France, and wake up to a sight of the English fields.

They all three had diverse reasons for some satisfaction of mind, and the sea was calm. They slept well.

The ambassador, on phoning M. Samuel to inform him, with some bluntness of speech, that he had decided not to remain in France, had found this intimation received without protest, and even some apologetic regret for the experience that he had had. He mentioned that the Prefecture had ordered the arrest of Mr. Kindell, as though that were conclusive evidence that he had committed the crime. Mr. Thurlow said that it would take a lot to convince him that Kindell would be guilty of such an act, and M. Samuel replied that new evidence had come into the hands of the police, which the young man would find it very hard to explain. "Our methods here," he had said, as though mentioning an evident superiority over those of the Anglo-Saxon races, "usually drag out the truth, when we've got such a start as we have here."

Mr. Thurlow, though less than convinced, saw additional cause for satisfaction that he would not be further involved. Kindell was a relative. He could scarcely have refused assistance, had it been asked. But it had been offered and refused, and he had been inclined to make a grievance of that! Perhaps Irene was right. Perhaps Kindell's motive for silence really had been consideration for them. The idea almost reconciled him to the presence of that infernal valise which Irene had insisted on bringing. After all, he was doing something for the fellow, and at some risk to himself, though he did not think it was much. If Kindell meant that he should sign off on those terms, well, it might have been worse than that!

Irene was more worried for Kindell's welfare, and anxious as to what ordeal he might have to face from the French police, but she could not believe that he was in serious danger of conviction for a murder of which she was certain that he could not have been guilty.

Trouble he was certainly in, but she had some confidence that he would be equal to finding his way out. And whatever anxiety she might feel, she was less distressed than she would have been had he not given her (as she supposed) an opportunity to atone for the way in which she had left him that afternoon. There should be no doubt of the valise being safely delivered! She would take it herself.

Professor Blinkwell had, perhaps, the most absolute peace of mind, for which he may have had the best cause.

He felt a degree of confidence almost equal to that of the ambassador and his daughter that the valise would pass the Customs without inspection, though he had a better knowledge of the risk it ran, and the trouble which would follow if it should engage the attention either of the Customs or the police. But in any case, he need have no personal fear. It was Gustav who would be questioned—and Kindell or perhaps the Thurlows who would be under suspicion. What on earth would it be to do with him?

And there was some satisfaction in having left the scene, and the country, of the murder of one who had certainly been a particular enemy of his, without having been drawn, even remotely, into the orbit of the crime. But then, who knew of that enmity? He was not even sure that M. Samuel had known that it was he whom he pursued. If he had, it had become improbable that he had shared his knowledge with others, or surely the police would have paid more subsequent attention to him! So it was reasonable to think. But the murder had made it additionally desirable that he should get safely away, and particularly that he should have no further connection with that of which the Thurlows had so obligingly taken charge.

His anticipation proved to be no more sanguine than was justified by the event. He had the satisfaction of observing the Thurlows leave Victoria station in their own car, piled with luggage, among which he had no doubt that the valise was unobtrusively included. Evidently no untoward incident had delayed them at the Customs. Actually, the ambassadorial privilege had prevailed, and their baggage, as they would have called it, had not been inspected at all.

Professor Blinkwell called a taxi, and was soon enjoying the pleasant comfort of a late breakfast at his own table.

It was a meal at which Mrs. Blinkwell, whose occupation, if any, was that of a professional invalid, did not appear, but Myra was there. And though the Professor was blessed (as he would have agreed) with an incurious wife, his niece was somewhat more in his confidence, and more alert to circumstances, in her lazy way.

Breakfast came first with her, but her plate being well supplied, curiosity had its turn.

"What's this," she asked, "about someone being found dead in Mr. Thurlow's room?"

"What, indeed?" her uncle echoed. "Am I to conclude that Kindell confided to you upon the boat?"

She looked at him with an irritation which had some cause, but a long experience of his conversational methods controlled her reply: "He didn't tell me anything. All I know is from last night's papers."

"Which I have not seen."

"But I expect you know more of what happened than got into them."

"On the contrary, I may know less. What did they say?"

"They said a detective officer had been found killed in Mr. Thurlow's suite in the hotel. They made quite a splash."

"I expect they would. Did they mention Mr. Kindell at all?"

"No, what was it to do with him? I was going to tell you that he gave me the slip at Dover. He stayed in the Customs House, and I didn't see him get on to the train. I was afraid something might have gone wrong about the parcel he was bringing for me, but, if there was, I heard nothing more about it, so he didn't give us away."

"He told me that he had very little difficulty in dealing with that matter."

"You've seen him since you got in?"

"No, I saw him in Paris before I left yesterday."

Myra stared at that. "But you can't have done. He came over with me."

"He went back that night."

"Why on earth did he do that?"

"He went at the request of the police. They thought the murder should be explained."

"But what was it to do with him?"

"That's what they want to find out."

"But—but that's absurd. He must have left before it happened."

"They seem to think differently. He was arrested yesterday afternoon."

Myra, whose feelings, unless for her own comfort or safety, were not easily roused, looked both troubled and bewildered.

"I could tell them that's nonsense."

"Which I must insist that you do not. We must not be mixed up in it at all."

Myra saw the prudence of this. Her protest was weak. She began, "But if—" and her voice fell.

"You need not trouble about him. He told me that he was in no way concerned, and, if that be so, his danger cannot be great. But there is something that you can do."

Hearing this, Myra did not look pleased. Her thoughts went to the parcel she had entrusted to him. Probably it might now be in the hands of the police. Did her uncle want her to claim it from them?

He saw the rebellion in her eyes, and read her thoughts as though they had been spoken aloud.

"Myra," he said, in a voice of patient remonstrance, "try not to be a bigger fool than you can't help. Do I ever ask you to do dangerous things? The parcel you gave to Kindell was opened by the Customs, and made no trouble at all. But the fact that it was opened gave me valuable information about Kindell, concerning whom I had been seriously misled."

"You mean he was letting us down?"

"On the contrary, I mean he wasn't. But I'm not asking you to think. There's something you can do without that being necessary."

Myra still looked mutinous. She cared little for her uncle's sarcasms, to which she was well used, but she cared much for her own lazy comfort, and for the maintenance of a satisfactory distance from the police, which she knew was not the invariable experience of all the members of the gang which he so adroitly controlled.

Unfortunately, the assurance of that lazy comfort came from the one who, from time to time, required her to undertake the dubious enterprises from which her caution if not her conscience sullenly rebelled.

It was true that obedience, intelligently though reluctantly given, had so far resulted in the immunity which he had assured her that she would have. But would it always be so? She saw danger now to be nearer than she had ever known it before.

Yet the professor's confusing half-explanation regarding the parcel with which she had been so reluctant to be concerned gave her some reason to rebuke her doubts. Had it really been of an entirely innocent character, and its only purpose to test Kindell's own character? It was so like her uncle to contrive such a scheme and to decline to say the explanatory word which would have relieved her of half her fears!

"You don't want me to claim the parcel?"

"Certainly not. If you should be questioned concerning it—which you need not anticipate, as it could only occur if Kindell should give you away, which is, for several reasons, highly improbable—you will repudiate knowing anything about it. Should you be shown the articles it contained, you will say, with absolute truth, that you have never seen them before. I may tell you that they are of such a nature that you will be readily believed. But he has said that he knew nothing of them, and you will find he will stick to that.

"It is in regard to a parcel of greater value that you can help me now and in an entirely innocent way, the safety of which even you will be able to see. I want you to go to Mrs. Collinson in the next hour—it is a position in which the only risk lies in delay, and even that risk is not yours—and tell her that the Thurlows have brought a parcel over for Kindell, and have been given her address to which to deliver it.

"She must take it in, and then telephone Braithwaite, who will fetch it without delay. I shall have prepared him for that.

"If any questions should be asked on its delivery, she must make it appear natural that he should have given her address. She can be his aunt, if she will."

Myra listened to these instructions in a natural bewilderment. Kindell was accused of a murder for which he could have no conceivable motive. He was arrested. He had taken charge, not this time of an innocent package, but of the illicit drugs which it had been so necessary, and had suddenly become so difficult, to get out of Paris and through the peril of the English Customs. He had asked the Thurlows to bring it. And, finally, he had given not his true address, but that of one of their own gang, for its delivery! She was to believe all that. And she knew that to ask for explanations was almost certainly to be rebuffed, or to be answered in some enigmatic way, by which her confusion would be increased.

"I thought," she said, "that you made it a rule that nothing should ever be done which would bring Mrs. Collinson under suspicion."

"So I have. That is precisely why she is useful now. And can you not see that it was necessary to give the Thurlows an address such as Kindell might naturally use?"

"Yes. I suppose it was. But I don't understand now...."

"And there is no reason why you should. But if you lose time, you may be late, which you must not risk."

"Shall I phone her first?"

"No. It is highly unlikely that she would be overheard. But it is a risk which there is no reason to run. There is no probability that the delivery will be made in haste. It is improbable that it will be today. But probability is not enough. I prefer to be sure."

Myra rose at that, and with as much expedition as it was natural to her to use she put on her hat, summoned a taxi, and proceeded to the address which was on the label which Irene had transferred to her own bag.

The hour being still early, and Mrs. Collinson being a lady of an indolence which even Myra could not rival, she was at home, but, having breakfasted in bed, was in process of dressing. They were known to each other, but not with the degree of intimacy which puts all ceremony aside, and so Myra must wait.

When the lady appeared, Myra came straight to the point, losing no time, as she was afterwards able to say in her own defence, to which there was no reply.

She had, in fact, a dislike for Mrs. Collinson which probably had its origin in a similarity of slothful selfishness which either could condone in herself rather than tolerate in another. She had no inclination to say more than was required by the errand on which she came.

"Professor Blinkwell," she began, "wants you to undertake something rather different from what you've been doing. There's a Mr. Kindell who has been told to give this as his address, and there's almost certain to be some luggage coming for him today or tomorrow. It won't be a lot. Just a suitcase, or something like that.

"All you have to is to take it in as though you expect it, and then phone Dulwich 7171—I've got it written down here for you, but it's best burnt—to say that you want the dressmaker to call as possible, and a lady giving the name of Bryant will fetch it away."

Mrs. Collinson looked worried. "I thought," she said, "that it was understood—"

"Yes, that you should not be required to do anything to draw suspicion in your direction. You know how strictly we've kept to that. And that makes it quite safe now."

"Of course, it's—"

"It's always best not to know. But you can be sure Professor Blinkwell wouldn't ask you to run any risk. Your banking facilities are too valuable for that. And then knowing him as you do...."

Mrs. Collinson considered that, and her face cleared. She was one of those who unavoidably knew that Professor Blinkwell controlled the gang, which few who took the major risks of their illicit traffic were permitted to do. What they did not know they could not disclose. And she was one of those who transmitted funds. She had no other activity. No, he would not be likely to involve her in any risk which would destroy her usefulness, and might even lead to his own betrayal. She said cautiously, "If I do this, I shan't be asked to again?"

"No, I don't suppose so."

"I hope that will be clear. Will there be any carriage to pay?"

"No, I should think not. Not much, anyhow."

"It isn't anything from abroad?"

"Oh, no! But its owner told you that he might send you such a case to take care of for him any time if he were going abroad."

"What name did you say?"

"Kindell...William Kindell."

"I seem to have heard that name somewhere." Mrs. Collinson looked puzzled, and then as though recollection came, and was succeeded by fear: "Isn't that the name—?"

"Mr. Kindell has been very stupidly arrested by the Paris police. All the world knows that. But it's nothing to do with...what interests us. And, in any case, he's quite innocent. I shouldn't wonder if he's released by now."

Mrs. Collinson showed no satisfaction as she listened to these assurances. She naturally concluded that Kindell was one of the gang, and had been actively engaged in the smuggling side of the business, when, whether guilty of murder or not, he had fallen into the hands of the Paris police. Thinking that, she became one more of those who were misinterpreting the risks they ran.

Myra had a fear that she was to meet with refusal, and perhaps be blamed by her uncle for the degree of frankness she had shown. Yet how could she have avoided that?

But Mrs. Collinson reflected that £800 of a total income of less than £1,000 came from the financial services she rendered. A refusal might risk it all. Further, she had a shrewd thought that as the valise had already been directed to her; to refuse it might lead to an investigation which would involve her in more risk than there would be in taking it in.

"Very well," she said. "I'm sure Professor Blinkwell knows what he's about. But it's not a thing you must expect me to do again."

Myra rose, with a feeling of relief at her success, making her almost sincere in the cordiality of her parting words. She saw, with satisfaction, that Mrs. Collinson, after glancing again at the slip of paper she held, put it into the fire. It was an easy number to remember. "Bryant," she said, "yes, Bryant."

Myra came away feeling that it had taken a long time, but she had done well.

As she left the gate, a large car approached. Irene was beside the driver. She was looking out. The eyes of the two women met.

Irene turned to her companion. She said something to him, and the taxi quickened speed as it passed the house.

Myra stopped the next taxi she met and went home. Her uncle was out. When he came back in the evening, she told him what had occurred.

He said little. What was there to say? He could not blame Myra. He certainly would not have wished Irene to see her coming out of that gate. But it was an event of uncertain importance. Probably none. Unless, of course.... He left the matter till the next morning. Then he passed the word to a subordinate, who phoned Mrs. Collinson, and learnt that the dress for Mrs. Bryant had arrived safely.

CHAPTER XIX.

MR. THURLOW IS NOT PLEASED

MR. THURLOW FELT a natural satisfaction as the short drive to Grosvenor Gardens was completed, and he passed through the Embassy doors. He was not merely in England again; he was, by an international fiction, upon the actual territory of the United States. He was at home and secure. Even had he known the true origin and actual contents of the valise which he had been cajoled into taking under his protection (and he suspected the one as little as the other), he would have regarded it as an ended danger. Certainly no one would enter those sacred doors with any purpose of hostile search.

But that article of unsuspected criminality had never been a major concern, and when he sat down to a breakfast such as would have been served in his own land, he had scarcely finished his preliminary grapefruit juice before he opened *The Times* (it being his deplorable habit to read the newspapers as he ate, even though his daughter, the councillor of the embassy, and two secretaries shared the meal), and saw an account of yesterday's events in Paris, which, even as they were narrated by that unimaginative periodical, was unpleasant to read.

He observed an angle which he might have anticipated from the first, but to which he had not given adequate consideration. It was not William Kindell, a British subject of no political importance, who had been arrested for murder, it was the cousin of the United States ambassador. This, in itself, however derogatory, might be of no critical consequence. Ambassadors who are immaculate in their private lives and closer family associations may survive cousins of homicidal habits. Cousins are numerous. Human nature is frail. It would be inconvenient for many if investigations were too widely spread.

But it is inexpedient for ambassadors with cousins of this quality to allow them to commit crimes in their own suites. In the best embassies, it is not done. Even *The Times* showed (most decorously) that it was not unaware of that. It showed it, by implication, in the care with which it explained the difference between French and English judicial procedure. Mr. Kindell had been detained rather than arrested. He was invited to give satisfactory explanations to a *juge d'instruction*, which it might be supposed that he would be able to do. But if this were the attitude of *The Times*, what would the *Herald Tribune* be saying now?

He looked up from the paper and met the eyes of his Second Secretary. "Alders," he said, irritably, "don't look so damned sympathetic. I'm not going to resign because of the inefficiency of the French police. If anyone thinks that, they can guess again."

"I'm sorry, sir. I wasn't thinking anything like that."

"They're only bothering Mr. Kindell," Irene interposed, "because they can't find out what happened. He just came up to say goodbye, and was gone before anything happened."

"I wish I were—" her father began, and checked himself. He was shrewd enough to know that it was less simple than that, though he could not imagine any plausible explanation. But even here, among loyal friends, he felt that silence was best. Facts might be told, but speculations were best unsaid.

"I think," Irene went on, "I'll take that case round to Will's rooms this morning. I dare say you'll be able to drive me there, if the Bentley's not wanted." (She looked at Alders as she said this, and the young man showed no inclination to reject the proposal.) "It won't take half an hour."

Her father said: "You'd better not. Send it by carrier. There's no need for you to do it yourself."

But even as he spoke, he saw that his objection was influenced by his feeling of irritation against Kindell and anything to do with him, rather than prudent judgment. It would be far better for the case to be delivered in that way rather than trusted to servants, who would doubtless observe its address with curiosity and speculate as to what it might imply.

He had not yet decided whether he would champion Kindell as his near relative, adopting a challenging attitude such as might win the sympathy of patriotic Americans, or adopt an opposite attitude of repudiation. But whether he were about to blow hot or cold, Irene's would be the better way.

So when his daughter replied, "Oh, but I'd like to," in a tone which he knew meant that she would not be easy to change, he gave way, saying no more.

Irene was influenced by motives which she might herself have found difficult to analyse. She wished that what she had undertaken should be promptly and certainly done. She still had a feeling of regret for her parting words of the previous afternoon and a desire to do what she could to atone. But the motive of curiosity may have outweighed that of contrition. The address on that label her bag still held was not that of Kindell's rooms. It was one she had never heard him mention. There were a dozen possible explanations of innocent simplicity. But she would like to be able to make a guess at what the correct one might be.

So she went, and her father was shortly afterwards able to get what satisfaction he could (which was not much) from a polite enquiry which his First Secretary received from the private secretary of the Secretary for Foreign Affairs. Would His Excellency join him for lunch at the Foreign Office? His Excellency said that he would.

CHAPTER XX.

AN OLD BLANKET WILL DO

LORD GLASTON RECEIVED the representative of the great American Republic with a particular courtesy which he considered that the position required. He avoided the subject which was in both their minds until the meal was far advanced and they had discussed various matters of international importance, when he said, in the casual tone of one who relaxes to the observation of trivial things: "I was sorry to hear of the annoyance you had in Paris. I am sorry also about Reynard. I am told he was a good man. It was not very creditable to the French police to let such an incident occur, and to be unable to clear it up."

"But," Mr. Thurlow answered, "won't they say they are doing that? They have made an arrest, and I am waiting with interest to know what kind of evidence they will produce."

"Then I can tell you at once that there will be none. If you will regard it as confidential until an announcement will be made by the French authorities—which they may not be quick to do—I will tell you that Mr. Kindell is already released."

"I am glad to hear it. You can, of course, rely upon my silence until I hear of it in other ways. Have they found who the murderer was?"

"No. It is less than that. But I may tell you in the same confidence that Reynard was on the track of an international drug-smuggling gang, and, though he was reticent in the details of what he did, there is little doubt that it was on that business that he visited your hotel, and that he was murdered by those who felt that he was too closely upon their heels."

"That is likely enough. But what I fail to see is why he should have entered my room, or they should have encountered him there."

"That is more than I can explain. But I can tell you that Mr. Kindell is under no suspicion. We have had a full report on the whole affair from the Bureau de Sûreté through Scotland Yard; and I will ask you this, which it might be useful for them to know. There were English visitors on the floor below you—Professor Blinkwell and his niece. Blinkwell is an analytical chemist, with commercial interests in manufacturing chemical works. His name is well known in this country. He has been suspected for some time past of being engaged in such traffic, but, if the suspicion be correct, he has been too circumspect for detection. Did you observe that he had callers while he was there, or—in short, did you see anything of him or his niece at all?"

Mr. Thurlow considered the possible results of a full reply to this question, and then answered with hesitation. "My literal reply must be no, but I am anxious to do everything in my power to assist the investigation, and I will add that my cousin might possibly be able to give you more information."

"I think they know that already."

"Then I cannot help you. The only time I recall seeing Blinkwell in conversation at all, it was with a member of the hotel staff and it would be absurd to see anything sinister in that."

"It was not a long conversation?"

"I could not say. It terminated as I approached."

"It certainly sounds unimportant. But I will let them know. Could you identify the man?"

"I seldom forget men. He was a waiter named Gustav. It was the same man who…."

Mr. Thurlow checked himself, and then concluded, "…who moved some luggage for me when we left the hotel."

Lord Glaston did not appear to observe the check which had broken the course of the last reply. But he noted the name, and turned the conversation aside, after a confident prediction that it was not a matter by which it was likely that the ambassador would be further annoyed.

Shortly afterwards, Mr. Thurlow returned to the embassy, and it was while having tea with Irene that he learned that the valise of which she had undertaken delivery was still there.

She told him what had occurred, and added: "I suppose I was rather a pig, but it was just an impulse. I hardly knew why I did it, but I couldn't see, if it were going to the Blinkwells, why he didn't ask them to bring it."

She had expected her confession to be met with sarcasm or rebuke, and would, indeed, have gone out again to deliver the valise before her father's return had there been an available car. But he took it in a different way. He said: "There may be an answer to that.

Blinkwell couldn't have brought it through without its contents being seen."

"Why should he have minded that? But, all the same, I'd give something to know. It's as heavy as though it were solid bricks." This was an exaggeration, but it increased the ambassador's rising interest in the nature of its contents. He said: "I'll have a look at it before it goes out again." Within the next minute, a manservant, carrying it in by one hand, but with an obvious consciousness of its weight, laid it before him.

Mr. Thurlow tested it for himself. He looked at it with an active curiosity which brought an exclamation of protest from Irene, "You're not going to open it, are you?"

"You think I've no right to do that?"

"Of course we haven't."

"I know more about this matter than you. More, in fact, than I am able to say. But I'm not going to open it, all the same. What I shall do is to invite Kindell to fetch it himself."

Irene still looked troubled, but ceased to protest.

"I don't mind," she said, uncertainly, "if you do that."

"Williams," the ambassador said, "could you find a suitcase about this size?"

"Yes, Your Excellency."

"And two or three bricks?"

"Yes, Your Excellency."

Williams retired, and returned with a suitcase of different appearance but similar size, and a large fragment of coping stone which the ambassador approved. He asked for a piece of blanket in which to wrap it, and finally packed it in a manner which would render it difficult for anyone handling it to discover that the contents of the suitcase differed from that which it was intended to replace.

"We will send this," he said, "to Professor Blinkwell's address and see what happens."

"It mayn't be his address. I only saw that woman coming away."

"We'll have a look at the telephone directory."

The evidence thus obtained disclosed that Professor Blinkwell had a different address. The ambassador rang for a street directory, and gained the further information that Mrs. Collinson occupied the house to which the valise was to be taken.

"Will may have rooms there, for all we know," Irene suggested, still disposed to defend him from others, while reserving him for her own attack.

"A young man doesn't need two sets of rooms."

"No...but there may be a simple explanation we haven't guessed."

"Then I shall like to hear what it is. And, till I do, the less you see of him the better I shall be pleased."

"I'm not likely to see much of him while he's in a French jail."

"No, but you don't even know that."

Having said this, Mr. Thurlow closed the conversation with some abruptness, on the plea that he had correspondence with which to deal. He was conscious that his last remark had approached disclosure of the information which he had accepted as confidential. Beyond that, he wished to give consideration to the new facts—if such they were—which he had learned during the day. The French police had satisfied themselves of Kindell's innocence—or, at least, that they had no evidence of his guilt—and had let him go. But that was not to be generally known Why? There must be a reason for that.

And their acceptance of his innocence might not go beyond the murder of which he had been explicitly charged. There was suggestion now of criminality of another kind. How did he stand about that? And how would he stand if the method by which he had sent that valise should be disclosed, and that it had been addressed to a place to which Blinkwell's daughter went?

The ambassador saw that there was a simple answer to these questions. *Everything* (as he saw the facts) would depend upon the nature of its contents. He resolved that Kindell should open it in his presence, or, if he should decline, the whole circumstances should be communicated to Scotland Yard.

Feeling that he had the situation in hand, and that there was little remaining probability of such developments as would cause trouble in Washington, which was naturally his major concern, he turned his mind to the international affairs with which it was his duty to deal.

CHAPTER XXI.

AN ERROR WITHOUT EXCUSE

KINDELL RETURNED TO London by air, on an understanding that he should not be seen in his familiar haunts, nor make contact with his friends. The sleuths of law were hunting on a cold scent which at any moment might become hot. It was important to confuse those whom they sought to catch. Let them think him still in the grasp of the examining magistrate—the one chosen by the police to expiate the worst crime of which policemen know, the murder of one of themselves.

Kindell might be of some immediate use, and at any moment a position might develop in which he could be of much more. But it was emphatically understood that he was to lie low.

His action in telephoning Irene cannot therefore be condoned. He did evil, and it was not even a doing of evil that good might come. Or, at least, the good, if any, was to be of a private sort, having no connection with the business he was engaged to do. The consequences, which he was far from foreseeing, cannot therefore be a logical credit to him. Yet, whether for evil or good, his action was of momentous bearing on the events that followed.

Irene picked up the phone in her own room (she had a separate line, intended to ensure the privacy of embassy conversations, rather than hers), and the temper in which she answered was not good, for her wristwatch, which she was putting on as the bell rang, slipped to the floor, having been insecurely clasped.

"Yes, who is it?"

"Is that you, Irene?"

"Yes, who's that?"

"Are you quite alone?"

"Who is that?"

"I want to know whether you're quite alone."

"And I want to know who you are."

"Can't you guess?"

"I don't see why I should...it isn't Will, is it?"

"You're not being overheard?"

"Considering I'm in my own room, and it's between seven and eight—"

"Will you meet me somewhere for lunch?"

"It really is Will?"

"Yes. But I wish you wouldn't keep saying my name."

"What's the mystery?"

"I'm not supposed to be here. What I asked was: can you meet me for lunch? And not let anyone know?"

"I might, if I knew why. Where shall it be?"

"You know where we met the Tuesday before you went over to Paris. Say a quarter to one?"

"You mean at—"

"There's no need to say where," he interrupted sharply. "And there's no need for me to come, if you can't—"

"I'll be waiting there. Right at the back."

He rang off abruptly.

Irene picked up her watch. She looked rather pleased with the world when she heard that it still ticked, but she frowned uncertainly over the proposed appointment. Had he discovered the contents of the substituted suitcase? How much had she to excuse or explain? Were they to meet as friends, or would they continue the quarrel in which they parted?

Well, he had approached her! She debated with herself whether she would go, but she knew all the time what the answer would be. Curiosity alone would have been enough to direct her steps. And there were other deeper, less acknowledged feelings which would be even more potent. But it was uncertain, when they should meet, what her mood would be.

So, with some restlessness of impatience, the morning passed, first in dressing to go out with more than her usual care, and then in desultory shopping until the hour came at which she could turn into the Norfolk Restaurant and make her way through the well-occupied tables to the dim-lit corner at the back where she had no doubt that Will Kindell would be.

"I thought," she said lightly, "that you were to be guillotined about now," and was then unsure as to whether her words had a heartless sound in respect of what might have been a real trouble to him.

But he took it in the right way. "No such luck for you," he returned, in as light a tone, "but I'm not out of the wood yet. I'm loose on something like a ticket of leave, and on condition that I find out who the real murderer is."

Irene frowned over this somewhat fanciful description of his position. "I don't see," she said, "how you can hope to do much about that here."

"On the contrary," he replied, "I believe that London's the place where the secret lies."

"And so you begin your investigation with me?"

He saw the implication of that. Had he meant that her father was the one to answer the question of who the murderer was? But he must tease her a moment with an oblique reply.

"Yes," he said, "I couldn't do anything till I'd started with you."

"I'd like to know what you mean by that."

"I mean that I can't concentrate on anything else till I know that we're friends again."

"Oh, you meant that!" She looked at him with a renewed kindliness in her eyes. But the next moment her mind recurred to the substituted suitcase, and the explanations that it required upon either side. "I think," she said, "you'd better see my father as soon as possible."

"I don't think I can. I'm not supposed to let anyone know I'm here. I ought not to have phoned you, but there are some things that can't wait."

"It's not much use seeing me if you're going on making a mystery of everything. And you really ought to see Father. It's about that case. There's something he wants to explain, and you ought to know."

"About what?"

"About the valise that you asked me to bring over for you."

Kindell controlled the astonishment which, for a moment his eyes revealed. He asked quietly, "Did you bring it?"

"Yes. But it hasn't been delivered yet. Not properly. But Father said he'd rather see you himself to explain."

"It won't be delivered till he has seen me?"

"Oh, no. You can be sure of that."

"Will your father be in now?"

"Yes. But he doesn't see anyone in the afternoon. He always works in his own room."

"I think he'll see me."

"He won't till evening."

"I think he will."

Irene, who had an approximately accurate vision of her father stretched on a couch, and dozing while *The Three Star Ranch* or *Quick-Trigger Jake* slipped from his hands to a quiet bed on the fireside rug, did not argue the matter further. They ate a lunch to the quality of which they gave less heed than it deserved, and with some pauses of silence on either side. When it was done, Kindell called a taxi, and they went back to the American Embassy together.

CHAPTER XXII.

Mr. Kindell Takes It the Right Way

IRENE SAID LITTLE on their way to the Embassy, and found that her companion had become equally silent. She preferred that her father should disclose the substitution for which he was responsible and for which, as the moment for explanation came, she felt that there had been no adequate cause, and therefore no tolerable excuse. On his side, Kindell, though puzzled to guess what could have occurred, was unwilling to show his ignorance until it had become less. He was anxious not to talk, but to hear.

"If you don't mind waiting till tea-time—I can make it a quarter to four if you like—Father will join us. But you don't know how angry he'll be if we disturb him now. He'll say there was no occasion at all."

"I don't think he'll say that. But I'll go up to him myself if you like, and you needn't come into it."

"I don't think that would be the best way. If you'll only say what the hurry is—"

"If I understood correctly, you said that you had undertaken to deliver something for me, and that your father had prevented it being done."

"Yes. that's what he did. He said he'd explain to you himself."

"Well, I'm here to hear it."

"But you'll only make him angry if you won't wait."

"I'll risk that."

"Well, I'll do what I can."

Irene went to her father's study, and found him dozing over a book, much as she had foreseen, but he rose at once when he heard who was there, showing as much alacrity for the interview as Kindell could have desired.

"How much have you told him?" he asked.

"Nothing. I said you'd explain everything. He seems rather cross."

"And frightened?"

"No, not a bit."

"Well, perhaps I've got to do some apologizing. But I don't think that's likely. I wish I did."

"Shall I ask him to come up?"

"Yes, of course."

"And you'll let me stay?"

"Yes. You'd better know what the truth is. There's nothing secret with us. Fetch him in, and tell Williams to bring that case."

The ambassador greeted his young kinsman with more cordiality than he had intended to show. He was not easily reduced to nervousness, but he was a shrewd judge of the demeanour of others, and he was conscious that Kindell's attitude was not that of one whose criminality is likely to be exposed. Still he knew what he had been told, and had not been free to repeat—and its inferences were clear.

Naturally, Irene had not understood, as he had been unable to tell her. But she soon would.

"I'm glad," he said, "to see that you've got out of the hands of those French police; but it was about this valise I wanted to see you. Can you tell me why it was to be delivered to Mrs. Collinson, instead of to your own rooms?"

Kindell had intended to conceal his ignorance until he had learnt enough to judge of the position with which he would have to deal, but this question was beyond the possibility of such a reply as would not imply all that he was reluctant to say. He answered simply, "No."

Mr. Thurlow felt that he was rebuffed in a manner which would be improbable had there been any natural and innocent explanation to give. It led him to a more abrupt challenge than he would otherwise have made.

"Do you mind opening it here, so that I may see its contents?"

"Why should I do that?"

"Because, in my official position, I cannot take the risk of being made the medium of anything which, for all I know, may be contrary to your country's laws."

Kindell restrained an inclination to retort that it was a scruple which came late. He asked, "Would you mind telling me how this came into your hands?"

"You mean that you thought Irene would bring it without my knowledge?"

"No, nothing of the kind. I am genuinely curious to know how it was brought either to you or her."

"Gustav brought it. Surely you should know that."

"I don't even know who Gustav is."

"Possibly you may not have heard or recall his name. He was the waiter by whom you sent it."

"Was he a sandy-haired man with particularly colourless eyes and a pointed chin?"

"It sounds like an accurate description. But what I asked was whether you would open the case."

"I could not do that without bursting it. I have no key, and it has the appearance of being strongly locked."

"You talk as though it were not yours. Would you be willing for it to be opened by the police?"

"It is what I was about to propose. My only hesitation is consideration for you."

"Why for me?"

"Because I think you have allowed yourself to be used as a medium for illegal smuggling, and I cannot tell how much would become public, or what effect it would have."

"Am I to understand that you threaten me unless I let you have it unopened? If so, you are wasting breath. I will call the police at once."

"Will you believe me if I tell you that I am working with them?"

"So I have understood. But it is possible that you may still have connections of which they are not fully informed."

"If you will tell me how this valise came into your hands, and why you have retained it, I will be equally frank with you, and you shall then be the one to decide whether you will call in the police or hand it over to me."

"You ask me seriously to believe that it was not sent by you?"

"It is the truth, and it will save time if you do. And time may be of more importance than I can explain briefly. That is why I insisted on disturbing you as I did."

"It was brought by the waiter, Gustav, with what purported to be a message to Irene from you, asking that it should be delivered to an address in London, which we have ascertained to be that of a Mrs. Collinson."

"And you decided not to deliver it?"

Irene interposed for the first time: "That was my fault, not Father's. I drove up to the door, and that Blinkwell woman was just coming out, so I drove away."

"Did she see you?"

"Oh, yes, she had a good look."

"Why should that make you suspicious?"

Irene looked confused at this question. "It wasn't exactly suspicion. I just felt that there was something wrong."

Kindell looked at her with an appreciation which she had not expected, and certainly did not deserve. "You were right there. But we've got to act quickly now. What I can't understand is that there's no address—no label on it. Did you have the address in writing? There might be a great help in that."

"There was a written label, but I took it off, so that it should appear to be part of our own luggage."

"Yes, but you kept it? You might let me see it now." Irene looked at her father, and he at her. Neither of them was as sure now as they had been before of the wisdom or justification of what had been done. Kindell noticed that he was not being held to his offer to give explanations to equal theirs.

Mr. Thurlow gave the reply: "I'm afraid we can't do that. I put it on to another suitcase, and sent it to the lady with about the same weight of stone inside. I reckoned that if it was all straight, someone would soon be at the door, and, if it wasn't, those concerned would get what they deserved."

But Kindell was on his feet. He said, "May I use your phone?"

Without waiting for a reply, he picked up the receiver. Mr. Thurlow heard the familiar number of the Foreign Office, and then, "Put me through to—" the speaker's voice fell, and "I7B" was the next articulation distinctly heard.

After that, Kindell's two auditors had the chastened satisfaction of hearing an account of their own proceedings, which, though concisely accurate in its facts, was generously imaginative in regard to the motives from which they sprang. Irene heard: "When Miss Thurlow saw Miss Blinkwell come out, she guessed something was wrong, and she had the presence of mind to drive on without stopping. Yes, I'm afraid she did, but that couldn't be helped. They couldn't make much of that. But when Mr. Thurlow heard what had happened, and that she had been seen, of course, he couldn't be sure till he could get in touch with me, that there was anything wrong; but he wouldn't take any risk, and he sent a dummy suitcase, just changing the label. Yes, it's still here. Wait a moment, I'll let you know."

Kindell broke off to enquire for Mrs. Collinson's address, gave it, and was then occupied in some exchanges which suggested that the brilliance of the ambassador's action was more apparent to himself than to the gentleman to whom he spoke; and that Kindell was resisting that criticism by pointing out, first, that any delay that had occurred originated in his own detention by the French police, a subtlety for which he was not responsible, and, second, that it had been reduced by his own initiative in getting into touch with the embassy in excess, if not in contradiction, of the orders he had received.

He hung up to say: "They want us to stand by and do nothing till they call up again. They'll be getting through to Paris now to deal with the Gustav angle. I don't suppose we shall have to wait long."

Irene said, "I think the best thing I can do is to ring for tea."

CHAPTER XXIII.

MR. THURLOW MUST GIVE WAY

"THE FACT IS," Kindell said, as the maid withdrew, and Irene picked up the teapot, "you did more for us, when you saw Miss Blinkwell come out of the house, than all the detectives in London or Paris had been able to do for the two years that we've had the investigation in hand. It makes this difference, that we can be sure now, where we only suspected before. But the question is: does it do more than that? It's not much use being certain of something you can't prove. And we've got to handle it now in such a way, if we can, that we pin something on to Blinkwell that he can't shake off."

"I can see now," the ambassador said, "that I made a mistake when I sent that false suitcase, though you were good enough to try to twist it another way. But I'll own that it never entered my mind that the message might not have come from you, and I wasn't willing to admit all the implications of that—not, at least, till you'd had a chance of clearing it up."

"I don't know," Kindell replied doubtfully, "whether it's going to turn out the right way or not. It depends, more or less, upon how quick they are in finding out what you had done, and how quick we can be now. And besides, if you'd let them have the right one, it might have disappeared beyond trace by now, and—no, we can't say what would have happened if you'd done it another way."

"A good deal," Irene said, "must depend upon what they get out of Gustav in Paris."

"Yes, if anything. There's always the doubt in these cases whether it's better to pick the man up or let him run loose a bit longer without knowing he's being watched; but with what we've got to go on now, both in Paris and here, they may decide that the time for action has come. We shall probably know a lot more when the telephone rings again."

As he said this, the bell rang, and he was soon hearing the voice of authority pronounce its verdict upon what had happened and suggesting—for it went beyond what could be ordered—what should now be done.

"Yes," he said at last, "we can try that. If I don't call back, you'll understand that that's how it will be."

A moment later he hung up, and turned to his companions to say, "They want us to deliver the right valise, and say we made a mistake."

Mr. Thurlow showed no enthusiasm for this suggestion. He said: "I don't see how you can do that...it's a bit late, anyway."

"We can't help that. We've got to act as fast as possible now. It's quite likely that the mistake hasn't been discovered. It all depends upon who had the right—and the key—to open it. You can be sure that it has a good lock. We shall find that out if we try to pick it. It's most likely that it would be necessary to break it open, and, if it's delivered intact, that may be taken as strong evidence that there's no suspicion of its contents.

"I suggest that whoever takes it explains that you took the label off while it was being passed through the Customs, and that it was then put back on the wrong case by a very easy mistake."

"That sounds all right," Irene agreed; "but it wouldn't explain why I drove away without delivering it."

"Probably not. But would explanation be necessary? You say Miss Blinkwell was leaving the house. We know she doesn't live there. She may not have gone back. Or she may not—"

"It doesn't matter. I know what I shall say. I thought the delivery of it was a private matter, and I didn't know how much Miss Blinkwell was in your confidence, so I just drove on. It was just an impulse—silly, of course, but that's how it was."

"Alders," Mr. Thurlow said, "can be furnished with that explanation, but I suppose it to be unlikely that he will be asked to give it."

"But," Irene answered, "I shan't leave it to him. I shall go myself."

"I shall certainly not allow that." Her father's voice was definite. "Of course, if Will likes to do it—"

"Unfortunately," Kindell answered, "I am explicitly forbidden to appear in the matter. They want Blinkwell to think that I'm being prosecuted in Paris, and that the police there are busy on the wrong scent. What we've found out now makes that all the more important. But I quite agree that it's a risk that Irene ought not to take."

Kindell felt, as he said this, the discomfort of one whom love and duty pull separate ways, for he knew that—particularly for her father's sake—Irene was the one who *should* take it, and he had express instructions to that effect, and a message he had not given.

"I don't see," Irene said, "that there's any risk at all."

"That," her father replied, "must surely depend upon whether the suitcase we sent has been opened. They wouldn't believe anything you say if they've seen what it contains."

"I needn't go into the house, if I don't want."

"All the same, Alders will go, and not you."

Kindell thought: "After all, would there be any real risk? And she's right that she needn't go into the house. If they've opened the suitcase, they'll be in a panic. They won't try to make things worse by doing anything to her. And they wouldn't be expecting her to call. It would be an utterly unforeseen development."

Beyond that, he was obliged, by the explicit instructions he had received, to object to the plan which was now proposed.

"The Foreign Office," he said, "are very anxious that you should not be officially involved in any further development."

"But if Irene—"

"It is not quite the same thing. In the first instance, the bogus message was directed to her. It is a matter with which your embassy might not be connected at all. Just a thing she did on her own, out of friendship for me."

Mr. Thurlow saw the force of that. Indeed, it not only might be, it was. And, but for his own interference—foolish interference, it might be said—so it would have remained.

Yet, in view of what was now known, for one of the embassy secretaries to be the medium of delivery, and perhaps, as a consequence, have to give evidence in court—well, it might still be steered in the right way. His agile political mind saw it being given such a twist that he might be applauded for the help he had given to the country to which he was accredited in rooting out a gang of international criminals. But he did not like it. It was full of risks, such as successful politicians must have become adroit to avoid. And the Foreign Office evidently saw it in the same light. They were willing to help him to pull out. It would be his own fault, if he should become further involved.

He saw another angle. He saw that, if Irene should be in the front of the picture, and especially if there should be a love interest suggested, however vaguely, between herself and Kindell (in his altered character of a Government agent), the chivalrous American public might be won to a most satisfactory sympathy. Every weight was in the same scale. But he was of no mind to buy his own advantage at his daughter's peril. He said, "All the same, I'm not willing for you to go."

"Oh, Father, you make me tired! The real question is how quickly I can get off, and which car I shall have."

"That's not the question at all. I'd rather cut the whole thing—"

"Anybody could see that you can't do that now. Or, at least, that this is the only way."

Kindell looked at two obstinate people, and had a sudden temptation to which he fell. At the worst, he would have an excuse. They were losing time, and there was unquestionable disadvantage in that. He had already acted with indiscretion in getting in touch with Irene, and its consequences were such that he would certainly escape blame. A second audacity might be equally fortunate. And there is no doubt that he found himself easy to convince, it being what he wanted to do.

"Suppose," he said, turning to the ambassador, for he was about to make a proposal which Irene would be unlikely to resist "that I go with her as far as the door?"

"You mean you would drive the car?"

"Yes, I might risk that. The Blinkwells don't live there, and the Collinson woman wouldn't know me."

"If they've not found anything out," Irene said shrewdly "it isn't likely that the Blinkwells would be there, and, if they have, I should say it's less likely still. And no one would think of looking to see if Will's in the car."

They all saw that. It would be the utterly unexpected again. Mr. Thurlow, half convinced, or rather wholly convinced, but still reluctant to agree to Irene's part in the matter, said doubtfully, "Well, if you're sure it's the best way—"

Will said, "I really think it is," and Irene was already getting through to the garage. "Yes," they heard her say, "the Austin will do. There'll be no one needed to drive."

CHAPTER XXIV.

PURSUIT

IT HAD BEEN agreed that it would be best for Irene to sit behind. She would be less conspicuous herself, and Kindell would have the appearance of driver rather than companion. He looked back over his shoulder to ask, "Can you describe the house, so that I can approach it without hesitation?"

"Yes. It is the second on the left of a row which have flights of steps in front, and porticos with white pillars. You'll see it easily."

"Steps? You think you'll manage alone?"

"I call that rude. If Father heard you, there'd be an international incident. What do you think American girls are?"

"What are they? Hydraulic cranes? You promise you won't go in?"

"Well—not unless we agree I shall."

"How do you propose to consult me, while I'm in the car?"

"If they press me to go in to change the cases inside, I shall say, 'Very well, but I must tell my chauffeur to wait,' and I'll run back to you; and if things look fishy I'll hop in, and we'll drive away."

"Yes. That ought to—sit back, so that you can't be seen from the house. CFS4602. Can you remember that? Can you write it down? I know this isn't the house. Have you got that number? Number 4602. Yes, that's right. But it's most likely a fake."

"You're going to follow it?"

"I'm going to try. It isn't easy in London streets. Not without giving the game away. Particularly not in this car, if they know only half of what they probably do. But we'll do what we can."

The abrupt change in the tenor of this conversation had taken place as they had turned into the square, and Kindell had driven the car up to the pavement fifty yards before that at which he had been directed to stop. He had done this at the sight of a low grey car standing before Mrs. Collinson's gate, and a man descending her steps carrying what, by an easy guess, was the suitcase which Thurlow had stuffed with stone.

Kindell thought hard, as he followed the grey car into Mostyn Road. He said: "Listen, Irene. We've got to pull this off, or we shall be almost back where we were, and your father'll get most of the blame. Gustav's going to stick it out that I really did send the valise to you, more likely than not, and you can see where we shall be."

"We shall be through the windscreen more likely than not, if you keep driving like that."

"Sorry. It couldn't be helped. Got any money?"

"Yes, three or four pounds. Why?"

"That ought to do. The next time I slow down at the traffic lights, I want you to slip out, so that they won't see you. Stop the first taxi you can, and follow me. Tell your driver to follow the grey car. As soon as I see you've taken up the chase, I shall turn off. I've got to get the police on the alert. That car can move, and even if we can't keep it in sight, I don't mean it to get away.

"But if you can keep on its track till it delivers the case, I want you to drop out then, get the nearest call box, ring up Scotland Yard, ask for Mr. Allenby—you'll find you'll be put through at once—and report to him. Tell your driver to keep on following the car, and not to lose sight of it till it's gone to earth somewhere where it's clear that it's putting up. Give him plenty, and tell him there'll be five pounds more for him when he calls at Scotland Yard, if he shows that he's got some brains. Have you got all that clear?"

"Yes. I think so. Mr. Allenby. Scotland Yard. Is that right?"

"Yes. Now out you go."

The next moment, he was alone.

So far the grey car had not been hard to follow. It was heading east, and there was nothing erratic in its course, nor any other evidence that its occupants were aware that they were followed. It was not going specially fast, and the traffic lights had been opportune for pursuit. So they were once again, as they enabled Kindell to close the intervening distance, so that there was nothing between them but a hooded van which concealed him effectually; and just as the red light changed a taxi drew up beside him. From it, Irene waved him farewell as it moved forward, and he delayed a second to note its number before taking the leftward turn.

Well, he must hope that she would have the luck to keep the swifter car under observation! But he was not depending upon that, or he would have kept the pursuit in his own hands. Within two minutes he was in a police telephone booth, and giving the information which would cast a swift net round the whole area within which the grey car must still certainly be. "They'll be lucky indeed," he thought, "if they put on enough speed to get away from Irene, *and* avoid the notice of the police."

But the voice of authority, which had directed him to hold on while it issued the orders which the occasion required, was now speaking again, "So you've still got the valise?"

"Yes."

"That's a pity."

"There was no possible time to deliver it without losing sight."

"Yes. I see that. It's a pity, all the same."

"Shall I go back, and do it now?"

"You've never met Mrs. Collinson?"

"No."

"Well, it's a risk. But it may be the best way. The drugs are of no use in our hands."

"They're bound to see the contents of the other one now."

"No, they're not. We may pick up whoever's got it before he has a chance to open it. If he does, they'll be puzzled as to what it means, especially if they have the right one handed over—and he mayn't have a chance to let Blinkwell know."

Kindell saw that there was sense in this argument. The fact was that the valise was of little use while it remained in their hands. Even against Gustav, it was not decisive evidence unless he could be proved to have known what it contained. To get it into the hands of those for whom it had been intended, and to arrest them after it had been opened, and when they were knowingly handling its illicit contents—it was at that they must aim, and, thinking this, he observed again how far from helpful the ambassador's action had been. But it was fair to him to remember that he had acted under a radical misconception of the position.

Anyway, his course was clear now. The only risk he could see was that he might encounter Myra, as Irene had done before, and, as he correctly guessed the position to be, the improbability of that was extreme. And he was no longer acting without official support, or actually against instructions, as he had done more than once in the last forty-eight hours. He went back to the car, and drove rapidly to Mrs. Collinson's residence.

CHAPTER XXV.

IRENE DOES NOT RETURN

A YOUNG MAID opened the door. She had a vacuous pretti-ness which did not suggest either that she was of a criminal kind or that she was one whom criminals would be likely to employ. She looked fit for the breaking of china, minor stupidities, or possibly pert replies. Nothing more serious would be likely to occupy or dis-turb her mind.

"I have come," Kindell said, "from the American Embassy. A suitcase was delivered here yesterday in mistake for this one. The labels got accidentally changed. Perhaps I had better see Mrs. Col-linson. His Excellency wished me to apologize and explain."

The girl's jaw dropped slightly. "I believe," she said, "as it's been taken away. I'd better tell the missus."

"If you please," Kindell replied, and the girl went to seek her mistress, leaving him at the open door.

She returned next minute, saying, "The missus says as it's noth-ing to do with her, but you can leave it if you've a mind."

But, as she said this, which, it may be safely assumed, was a very free rendering of Mrs. Collinson's actual words, that lady ap-peared behind her, having evidently decided that something was happening with which she should deal herself. She said: "That's all right, Becky. I'll see the young man myself." Becky retired, and Mrs. Collinson took her place.

Kindell said: "His Excellency wishes me to express his regret for the mistake which has been made. He wishes me to explain that the valise came as part of his own luggage, but Mr. Kindell had pro-vided a label to be used for its delivery to you, and that label was very carelessly put on to another suitcase."

Mrs. Collinson did not look particularly interested. She said: "Well, you're a bit late. He took it away half an hour ago. It's really nothing to do with me. But you can leave it, if you think that's the

107

best course. I daresay he'll come back when he finds he's got the wrong one."

"We are naturally anxious to get that one back," Kindell replied. "Don't you think you might telephone him and explain? He wouldn't be likely to see what was inside without bursting it open, and it would be a pity not to let him know what's happened before he does that."

Mrs. Collinson looked stubborn. She said at last, "Well, I don't mind you using my phone, if you think that would be any help.

"Thank you. If you will let me know his number, I'll get through at once."

"His number?" Mrs. Collinson looked surprised. "I've no idea. I scarcely know him at all. I've been puzzled as to why he used my address." And then, as one who was conscious of some cause for resentment, but did not wish to be unmannerly to those who were not directly concerned, she added: "But I suppose it would be in the telephone book. If you'd like to try that—"

She moved aside as she spoke, inviting him to enter, but he was not attracted by the comedy of ringing himself up at his empty room. He said: "I don't think that's really necessary. It would be going beyond my instructions. His Excellency might prefer to do it himself. If you would very kindly telephone us when the case is returned, we will fetch it without delay."

He had rested the one he had brought on a hall chair as this conversation proceeded. Now he withdrew his hand, and moved backward to the door.

Mrs. Collinson looked at it, he thought, for one doubtful second, as though she would prefer to tell him to take it away but other considerations prevailed. She called sharply to Becky who appeared from the end of the hall, and said to her: "You'd better let this stay here till Mr. Kindell comes for it. He's taken the wrong one. You'll have to see he leaves that, and we'll let this gentleman know."

"If he finds he's took the wrong one, we'll soon be hearing him at the bell," Becky foretold, and Kindell, having lingered to see as much as he could, withdrew with an added realization of how difficult it was to obtain conclusive evidence against the evasive tactics which these wealthy criminals so adroitly used.

His next action must obviously be to take back the car, and to excuse himself to the ambassador for returning alone. He was not entirely at ease on the last point, remembering the condition on which Irene and he had set out together, though he felt no apprehension for her safety, and felt that there was sufficient justification for the course he had taken.

But his doubt was soon removed when he found that Mr. Thurlow, after listening to his narrative in attentive silence, said with more cordiality than he had often shown him during recent days: "Well, I'd say you've made a good job of that. It sounds as though you've put the cops on the right track, and it won't be long before they'll be able to haul in the line."

"I was a little afraid," Kindell said frankly "that you might think that I shouldn't have let Irene go on alone But it was either that or...."

"It was either that or leaving her to take back the valise," the ambassador agreed, "and you'd got to put the cops wise, which you'd do better than she. I'd say you did it the best way, and Irene isn't a fool. Sitting in a taxi watching another car that doesn't know she's on its track oughtn't to be any headache to her. It isn't as though your toughs make a habit of shooting it out in the London streets."

Kindell's own mind, which was not entirely at ease, could not resist the soundness of this argument, and he was relieved that Mr. Thurlow took the matter in so sensible a way. He saw that to the American mind, there could be no ready recognition of danger in London streets. And it was mere recognition of the obvious to see that, whoever might be in the grey car, their first thought, even if conscious of observation, would be to avoid anything which would draw further attention to themselves. They believed themselves to have a very valuable and damning quantity of illicit drugs in their possession. Surely, their only thought would be to elude pursuit in the busy streets. Irene should be in no danger from them; and she was with a taxi driver whose number was known.

"Well," Kindell said, "I ought to ring up the Yard now, if you don't mind my doing it from here."

The ambassador waved his hand toward the instrument in reply. He said: "It's through to the exchange now. Go ahead." He was soon having the benefit of Kindell's part in a conversation from which it quickly became evident that something unexpected had happened—something that Kindell found it hard to believe, and that it was no pleasure to him to hear.

The connection being quickly made, Kindell asked, "Is that Superintendent Allenby speaking?"

"Yes. Where are you?"

"At Grosvenor Gardens. Yes, I'm with His Excellency now. I've delivered the valise to Mrs. Collinson. I handed it to the woman herself."

"Yes. We know that. What did you say was the number of the grey car?"

"CFS6402."

"Certain?"

"I was behind it for more than a mile."

"Well, it couldn't have been."

"Sorry. I don't mean to be rude, but I know it was."

"Will you describe it again?"

"Low, streamlined. Painted light grey. New. Looked as though it might have been in the showroom a week ago."

"Maker?"

"Couldn't say certainly from a back view. Starmar, four-seater de luxe, at a safe guess."

"That's the car, and it wasn't there."

"You mean the number was a fake?"

"They couldn't fake the car."

"It isn't easy to see how. But it was there, all the same. What makes you think differently?"

"We don't think, we know. A constable stopped it in Regent Street half an hour ago. It belongs to Rose Courtney."

"You mean *the* Rose Cour—?"

"Yes, the actress."

"Then it means she's in it, that's all."

"It doesn't mean anything of the kind. The car had been waiting outside the Lyric, while she'd been rehearsing for two hours. There are a dozen witnesses to that. Probably more."

"All the same, what I told you was right. You'll find Miss Thurlow will say the same."

"Is she home yet?"

"No. There's not been overmuch time."

"There'd have been lots of time if she'd been following that car till we picked it up. She hasn't been doing that since then."

"And she hasn't reported to you?"

"She certainly hasn't. And we haven't heard of any other grey car trying to get away."

"Well, when you do hear from her, you'll find that I wasn't wrong."

"Yes. I hope we shall."

"There'll be the taxi driver, as well as she."

"So there will. You'd better come here at once. And leave a message asking Miss Thurlow to ring us up quickly if she gets home before we've heard from her."

"Yes. I'll do that. I'll be with you in ten minutes."

Kindell put back the receiver. He turned to the impatient ambassador to say: "There's some fool muddle. They say the car belongs to Rose Courtney, and I must have mistaken the number. I'm not such a fool as that."

"They haven't heard anything of Rene?"

"Not yet. They want her to phone at once if she gets back here before she's reported to them."

"She wouldn't do that. Not on what you told me. She'd ring them up the moment she stops following the car."

"It looks as though it's been a long chase. But the police wouldn't let it get very far. I've got to go to Scotland Yard now, and make them get it into their heads that I didn't make any mistake. When they believe that, they'll have taken the first step to getting at whatever the truth is. Yes, I'll phone you the first minute there's anything to report. And you'll let me know when Irene gets back?"

"I sure will. But I'm not worrying about her. Rene knows how to look after herself."

Kindell hurried away. He thought, from the ambassador's tone, that he spoke rather to bring conviction to his own mind than because it was already there. And his own anxiety was not easy to keep under control.

When he had gone, Mr. Thurlow's demeanour changed. He frowned thoughtfully, muttering:

"It sounds a queer business to me."

He paced the room restlessly, as the minutes passed, and Irene did not return.

He reminded himself that the valise had gone. There was no longer any possibility that His Excellency the Ambassador of the United States to Great Britain would become notorious to an astounded world as a harbourer of illicit drugs. He must find satisfaction in that. And any escapade in which Irene might now be engaged was not of an official character. She was not even in an embassy car.

But he telephoned twice at short intervals to Scotland Yard for information they could not give, and when seven-thirty came and she was still absent, he irritably ordered that dinner should be held back, as, "Miss Thurlow may be coming in any minute now."

He pulled open a drawer in his desk and looked gloomily at an automatic which had been most often in his hip pocket when he had been in the livelier atmosphere of his Southern State.

But he closed it again without picking up the weapon. He had already been accused of driving a knife into a French policeman. Was he to make the idea credible by going gunning in London streets? And where would he propose to go? Well, Professor Blink-well would do for a start.

He had to remind himself sharply of whom, and in what country, he was. It was a land in which ambassadors' daughters were quite safe, even though they should elect to follow grey cars through its metropolitan streets. But if—well, he found some grim satisfaction from the thought that the gun was there.

CHAPTER XXVI.

PROFESSOR BLINKWELL DINES AND TALKS

PROFESSOR BLINKWELL DINED with his niece. His mind was more completely at ease than it had been at any time during the previous fortnight, and this serenity was not disturbed by the knowledge, which had reached him an hour before, that a second valise had been deposited at Mrs. Collinson's door. There had been plausibility in the explanation which had been given, and, in any case, two was much better than none

He had decided earlier that the peril which had come so unpleasantly close to his reputable and luxurious life had withdrawn to its customary remoteness, during which it had been no more than a vague shadow of which it was neither necessary nor comfortable to think. There had remained only the possibility that the ambassador might fail to make safe delivery of that which had been placed in his charge. A remote risk, and threatening Gustav and others rather than himself. But there was £6,000 at stake, and it is an amount which even men of wealth do not lightly lose.

Now all was well. So he said to Myra, whose duller mind had been somewhat disturbed by the news which she had been the means of conveying to him, after Mrs. Collinson had rung up a friend and engaged in a conversation which could have little meaning to anyone who should listen-in, which had been relayed to Myra in the same cryptic form.

"Suppose," she now said dubiously, "they opened it first?"

"It is a most improbable thing."

"I don't see that."

"No? Well, suppose they did?"

Myra was frequently reduced to puzzled silence when her uncle tossed the ball of conversation back to her in this manner. Now she said doubtfully: "Well, they'd know what was in it. They'd—they'd be watching it wherever it goes."

113

"Well, what of that?"

"Well, of course, suppose Mrs. Collinson gave you away?"

"We know she didn't."

"I mean if she should."

"You meant at some future time? Then why not say so? You know how I hate your slovenly English. I think it comes from listening to the news bulletins of the B.B.C."

"Well, suppose she should give you away?"

"The trouble with you, Myra, is that when you get frightened you can't think clearly. It is a dangerous fault. She won't give us away, because she'd have to give herself away first, and it is a sacrifice which she would be unwilling to make."

"What do you think she'll say?"

"I don't suppose she'll have occasion to say anything. But if she does, it will be that Kindell took advantage of a very slight acquaintance to dump the case on to her. He couldn't prove that he'd never heard of her before; and the fact that he didn't ask Thurlow to send it to his own rooms will seem natural enough. He sent it where it wouldn't be likely that it would be looked for, if they were on his track."

"Yes. I suppose that's how it would look," Myra replied doubtfully. Her uncle's elaborate fictions were often so sustained and detailed as to leave her mind confused at last between truth and falsehood. That being so, was it strange that they should deceive others who were less fully informed? "But," she added, "they won't believe much of that if he's in with the police."

"Which we have good reason to doubt. But, even then, it would be less than sure. As I said before, he might be running with hare and hounds."

"There's Gustav as well as Mrs. Collinson."

"Yes, there's Gustav. And he's an additional reason why you can sleep with a quiet mind. If the police here think there was anything wrong with the case, they'll ask Thurlow how he got it, and he'll say Gustav brought it with a message from Kindell. They'll question Gustav, and he'll confirm that.

"He couldn't bring me into it without accusing himself, and it's a safe bet that he won't. Not with Reynard's murder to be explained! Samuel's hauled in Kindell for that. Now if he finds that drug-smuggling was going on, won't he connect the two things? Who will Mrs. Collinson say has planted that case on to her? Kindell, whom she will admit that she slightly knew. And who will Gustav say gave it to him? Kindell again!"

"They mayn't believe Gustav's as innocent as he makes out."

114

"Very possibly not. They may decide that he was in with Kindell. They may begin to wonder whether he may not have been the one who got rid of Reynard, for which a waiter might have an excellent opportunity. They may confront Kindell and him, and if they find out the truth from what the two say, they'll be clever men. One thing is certain. Kindell will deny that he ever heard of Mrs. Collinson, and they'll find it particularly hard to believe that. Anyway, they'll have two to choose from, and if one of them's for the guillotine, Gustav would be my choice."

"You don't think he'd let it come to that without giving you away?"

"My dear Myra! How could he? Of course, he might bring my name in. But who'd believe him? He'd have said he got it from Kindell first. If that goes down with the police, he can't be the one to change. If they prove he's a liar, will they be ready to believe when he starts up with a new song?

"And by that time he'd be in it too deep to accuse anyone in a way that wouldn't involve himself. Do you suppose, even if they should believe him, they could do anything against me on the word of a confessed criminal? I'm not altogether sure that it wouldn't be a good thing if they *did* give him a taste of the guillotine. He knows rather too much, and he might be a nuisance before long."

"You don't think it really was he who killed Reynard?"

"I don't think about it, one way or other. I've got enough to do to think of my own affairs. There's a board meeting of Vantons tomorrow, which may be one of the most important we ever had, and they'll be expecting a report from me which is not ready yet. I'm thinking mostly of that."

Myra was not too foolish to see the implications of that reply. Professor Blinkwell was thinking of other things than a policeman's murder, or the distribution of evil drugs. People thought of other things when they thought of him as a director of Vantons Ltd., the great chemical firm, and the one on whose scientific advice the board of that firm relied. It was the armour in which he walked.

The butler entered. He came to the side of his master's chair. He said with the low-voiced expressionless intonation which good butlers use: "Mr. Tarleton is on the phone in the library, sir. He said he'd just heard from Siemans & Vie. He thought you might like to know."

"Thank you, Gilson. Tell him I'm at dinner now, but I'll ring him up in the morning."

The butler retired, and Professor Blinkwell looked at his watch. The message was a most natural one for such as he to receive. And

115

his reply showed that he did not regard it as of urgent importance. Siemans & Vie were a firm of manufacturing chemists in Berlin. They had business relations with Vantons which was legitimate and publicly known.

But the message was a code one which told him that a matter of urgency had arisen. It told him where it had occurred, and who would be on the phone (doubtless giving a false name) within five minutes, in the laboratory office on the floor below.

The butler, who understood more of what went on in that house than would ever pass his lips, brought, in the next minute, the coffee which concluded the meal, and the Professor, drinking expeditiously, but without evidence of haste, and saying nothing further to Myra (who understood the significance of that message as well as the butler, or perhaps better, but had learnt the wisdom of silence at such moments), went down to deal with whatever it might portend.

CHAPTER XXVII.

ACTION AT SCOTLAND YARD

AT EIGHT-THIRTY Mr. Thurlow considered that his continued refusal to have dinner served was making much of what he was determined to think was a small affair. At eight-forty he said that he had eaten all he required, and he telephoned to Scotland Yard again. This time, he was not told that there was no news. Kindell answered him, and his anxiety was evident in his voice. "There's one thing turned up, but you can't call it good, and it isn't easy to guess what the explanation can be. We only heard it a few minutes ago, and I was just going to ring you. The taxi's been found, but the driver's missing."

"You mean the car's been abandoned?"

"Not exactly, or at least not as though it were done in a hurry. It's standing on a cab rank off Holborn, but there's no one in charge. It was reported by another driver, who said it was obstructing the rank."

"You've no clue to what happened?"

"We're fetching it in now."

"There's no news of Rene?"

"Nothing here. I hoped she might have got home."

"Well, she hasn't. I can't understand how—"

"Superintendent Allenby wishes me to assure you that everything possible's being done."

"I can't agree about that. I'm coming over now."

The ambassador heard Kindell say, "He says he's coming here now," and then, a moment later, "Superintendent Allenby says he'll be glad to see you."

"Will he? I hope he'll have some better news for me than he's got now."

Mr. Thurlow rang off without giving time for reply. He ordered a car, and then turned to the drawer which he had opened before.

But this time the gun he handled was not laid down, but slipped into a hip pocket which readily adapted itself to a shape it had known before.

He gave a brief instruction that he was to be rung up instantly at Scotland Yard if Irene should return, and it was no more than a few minutes later that he was in the presence of Superintendent Allenby, and found that he had met a man whose efficient unhurried urbanity even his anxious impatience could not disturb. Being one who was not only efficient himself, but who could recognize that quality in others, he was also quick to recognize that everything possible *was* being done, and his manner changed.

"I am glad you have come," the superintendent began "because I should like you to know what steps we have already taken, and to hear any suggestions for further action which your experience and knowledge of those concerned may suggest.

"It is difficult, on our present information, to decide with certainty what has occurred, but there are certain indications which limit the scope of our enquiries, and should be of material assistance in solving the problem, even although we are dealing with particularly astute and unscrupulous men, who have the assistance that money gives.

"I should tell you first that we are proceeding on the assumption that Kindell really did make no mistake in the number of the car, and we are at least equally certain that the one that legitimately bears that number was standing outside the Lyric Theatre during the time that he was following a similar one in the Mostyn Road.

"You will readily see the implications of—"

He broke off as a clerk entered the room and laid a sheet of typed foolscap before him. "These are the particulars for which you asked, sir."

Superintendent Allenby's glance went rapidly down the page. His pencil ticked three of the list of names which it showed. "They must all be followed up," he said, "and without delay. Tell Chief Inspector Rolls that the three I have marked are worth special attention."

He explained, as the clerk withdrew: "That was a list of all the new Starmar cars of that pattern, size, and quality which have been sold during the last year. We are probing the possibility that someone has deliberately used a fake number plate identical with that of Miss Courtney, either habitually, or more probably, on particular occasions when occupied in illegal traffic. It is a device which shows the elaborate trickery of the men with whom we are concerned, and which might have caused more confusion and uncertainty than it has."

"I am surprised that you have been able to obtain the list so quickly."

"We had the secretary of the Starmar Company on the telephone. We contacted him at the Plaza an hour ago. He was good enough to ring up a managing clerk who lives within two miles of their Nottingham offices, and to arrange for him to go there and phone us the required particulars. They have come through half an hour earlier than I could reasonably have expected. A member of the Starmar staff would doubtless have a fast car! You may be sure," he added, "that we should allow no time to be lost in view of Miss Thurlow being concerned, though I should not wish you to think that we are seriously concerned for her safety. As I said before, the criminals with whom we are dealing are as astute as they are unscrupulous, and that astuteness would make them particularly careful not to interfere with anyone in Miss Thurlow's position."

"If she isn't home in the next hour, you can reckon she's being detained somewhere by force, and if that isn't interference—"

"I shall be inclined to agree with you about that, particularly as there is good reason to believe that the car cannot have gone far. Of course, I cannot vouch for the vigilance or for the intelligence of every member of the constabulary force of half a dozen counties round London, but unless there has been a remissness somewhere such as there is no reason to expect, that car did not get away for more than fifteen miles, and probably ran under cover somewhere very much nearer.

"This is rendered more probable—indeed, almost certain—by the fact that Peller's car has been found so short a distance away, and—"

"Peller being the taxi driver?"

"Yes."

"You don't think he could have been in collusion with them?"

"The circumstances make it improbable, apart from which Inspector Barclay, who deals with these drivers, says that he has known him for twenty years, and has confidence that he is a straight man."

"You're certainly picking up the threads. But doesn't the fact that he has disappeared, being a man of that character, make the whole thing look a lot worse?"

"I have no wish to minimize it. And I am disposed, as I have said already, to agree that, if Miss Thurlow is not back very soon, the probability that she is being detained against her will must be recognized. What I meant was that they will be very careful not to treat her with any disrespect. It is more probable that she would merely be prevented from communicating with us long enough for them to get away, or to remove incriminating evidence."

"And the driver also?"

"It is hard to reconstruct what has occurred from the material at present available. He may have had to choose between protecting his passenger and abandoning his car. It was evidently important to move it from wherever it was, which must therefore almost certainly have been near some premises occupied by members of the gang— presumably where the grey car is hidden—which it would have given away. The fact that it was not merely driven to a misleading distance, and abandoned there, but put on to a cab rank, suggests that it was considered important to delay its discovery as long as possible. It might have stood there for many hours without being reported to us. And that supports my suggestion that the detention of both Miss Thurlow and the driver—if that should be actually occurring—may be of a temporary character. But it is our business to make that time too short for their escape, which we may still hope to do."

Having said this, the superintendent switched his desk telephone to enquire as to whether Peller's car had been brought in.

So it had, but he was to gain no satisfaction from that. It was in good order. There was no slightest sign of any struggle having occurred, or any abnormality of any kind. It was just an empty car.

Thurlow said abruptly, "I suppose that fellow Blinkwell's at the bottom of this?"

The superintendent replied with caution. He did not forget that he had received direct instructions from the Home Secretary on the telephone half an hour earlier that he must keep the United States ambassador clear of further complications at almost any cost. He said: "There is a grave suspicion of that. He is being closely watched. He will be unable to go anywhere, or to write or telephone, unobserved, as long as this matter remains unexplained. But it may be very important that he should not know that he is suspected by us."

"Learnt anything so far?"

"Less than an hour ago, there was a telephone conversation between a man at a call-box and someone who spoke from Blinkwell's laboratories in the name of one of his staff, but who may have been Blinkwell himself. If it were so the conversation was intended to mislead anyone who should listen-in, but it would appear that something had been done at which Blinkwell was surprised and annoyed, and that he told the man who spoke to him that he must get out of his own mess in his own way."

"You'll have thought of sending someone to question him?"

"It would almost certainly be useless. He would deny everything. Professor Blinkwell is a very clever man. It would be we who would have given ourselves away."

"You wouldn't think to threaten him with a bullet in a nasty spot unless he should come clean?"

"No, we are not encouraged to those methods. Public opinion is troublesome in this country."

"But if I were to do it for you, it might give you a leg up?"

Superintendent Allenby knew that he would be blamed if he should permit that which he had yet no legal power to prevent. He judged also that Mr. Thurlow was not a man who would be easy to turn, especially where his daughter's safety was so nearly concerned. He showed his fitness for the position he held when he answered readily: "Yes. That might be worth trying. Your trouble would be that you couldn't carry out the threat if the bluff should fail. Certainly not on anything we know now." He went on hastily to the suggestion to which he had been leading, seeing an expression on his visitor's face which he would prefer not to hear put into words: "But I can make a better suggestion. We can send Kindell. It would be natural for him to call, and he can show his hand, more or less, as the occasion requires."

Mr. Thurlow did not reject the proposal, but he did not look pleased. He would far rather have gone himself. He was impatient for action, and he had some confidence in his powers of persuasion, supported by that which his pocket held. Yet he was not insensible to the difficulty which had been suggested to him. He could threaten Blinkwell with a bullet if he should refuse to talk, but what if he should call his bluff? If he should be obstinate, or even unable to give the information required?

Mr. Thurlow saw that the superintendent was right. He would be unable even to give the Professor an advisory bullet in a non-vital spot. Even had he been no more than a private citizen of the United States, his difficulty would still have been that, however strong his suspicion, he was not sure. As it was, with the responsibility of his official position upon his mind—no, it could not be done. Not even for Irene's safety. They must think of something better than that.

Yet he was slow to approve the suggestion that Kindell should go. He was still somewhat dubious of what his relations with Professor Blinkwell—his feelings towards Myra—might be. The doubt was slight, but it was still there. And there was also that of his ability to handle the situation. "You think," he asked, "that Kindell could pull it off better than I?"

"Kindell is one of our most trusted agents. He has already established such relations with Professor Blinkwell—and with his daughter—that it will be natural for him to call to let them know that he has been released by the French police."

"Very well. The sooner he gets started the better."

"Yes, for every reason. A midnight call would require more explanation than it would be easy to give."

As the superintendent said this, he phoned for Kindell, who had been waiting impatiently in an adjoining room to hear the result of this interview. There was a brief discussion of how it would be best to act under the varying circumstances which might confront him, and then Kindell, avoiding the use of an official car, set out on foot, and stopped the first taxi that cruised past him with a lifted flag.

As he was on the way, he considered that it was already late, and that the Professor might well decline to see him at such an hour. What should he do then? How should he force an interview which he would be unwilling to defer?

His plan was ready when he arrived at his destination, but it was not required, for Professor Blinkwell was as anxious for information as he. He said that he would see Mr. Kindell.

CHAPTER XXVIII.

SYLVESTER SNACKLIT IS NOT DECEIVED

SYLVESTER SNACKLIT HAD disliked the order from the first moment when it had reached him by the usual indirect telephonic method, and in the usual cryptic phraseology—cryptic, but plain to him.

He had his own place in the criminal gang to which he belonged. It was a place of importance, and it gave him congenial occupation. It was no less than what Mr. Thurlow's enterprising countrymen would have called the bumping-off of such individuals as became dangerous to the gang, or who committed breaches of discipline too serious to be forgiven.

What was done was therefore for the common preservation of himself and his friends. The law of self-protection approved it, and he could therefore indulge his own sadistic inclinations while his conscience remained at peace. Duty, profit, and pleasure would be at one, which is a more fortunate combination than will be experienced by most men who obey the law.

He had exceptional facilities for rendering these services to the organization to which he belonged. With some of the money left by his father (a philanthropist of national reputation) he had established the Snacklit Home, which received domestic pets of any kind, but was primarily a dogs' hospital and a dogs' home.

One of the most lucrative occupations of Snacklit Home was killing dogs. Dogs from all over London were brought to be destroyed there. They were brought by the police. They were brought by private persons—the kind of persons (mostly women) who would have their dogs killed because they were getting old, or had contracted some illness, or because they themselves were going abroad, and the poor things would fret if they were left alone.

But it was not spoken of as killing dogs. No kind-hearted woman could endure the thought of arranging to have her dog

123

killed—a creature which looked up to her with love and trust, and of which she was fond. They were not killed; they were put to sleep. Anyone can see the difference in that.

Cats also, many of them sleek and pampered, entered the same fatal door. They all gave pleasure to Sylvester Snacklit, but his high-water marks of happiness were when he could use his lethal chamber for human victims. So far, it had only happened three times in as many years. But there was always hope of what the next day might bring.

Apart from these occasional activities, for which he was promptly and liberally paid, his only services to the gang were in the initial stages of the distribution of the evil merchandise in which they dealt, and, for this brief and occasional purpose, his precautions against discovery included the disguising of the car which he openly and legitimately used, by the substitution of a number plate which would identify it as belonging to another owner.

He was one of the five living persons (if we exclude the suspicions of the police) who could have identified Professor Blinkwell as the head of the gang to which they belonged, and he knew enough of the methods which were in use to be surprised, and somewhat perturbed, when he received instructions to collect the valise from Mrs. Collinson's house. He knew that something must have gone wrong of sufficient seriousness to upset the basic rules of their organization.

It was not usual for him to make such collections himself, but, though not of a reliable courage, he had the temperament which, when alarmed, becomes impatient to force the event. He told Burfoot, the car driver and usual agent for such occasions, that he would go with him. He told himself that this would avert the necessity of giving Burfoot Mrs. Collinson's name.

He found the case waiting for him in that lady's hall, and received it from Becky's hands without ceremony or delay. It was of an expected weight, and it was not until he had settled down in the car, with it in the seat behind him, that he noticed that it was not of the pattern or quality which it was customary to use for these highly valuable and secret consignments.

He observed this first with curiosity rather than suspicion He had already accepted the idea that something unusual had happened. Doubtless this had involved the use of a makeshift receptacle. It would be part of the plan by which Professor Blinkwell's inexhaustible ingenuity had baffled investigation, as it had done so often before.

But then his attention became fixed upon the fastening of the case. It looked a wretched lock. A mere pretence, such as will be fitted to the cheaper suitcases, and that can be opened by almost any key of approximately the right size.

"It's ten to one," he thought, "that I could do it from my own bunch." His next thought was that it would be fortunate if he could, for it was evident that the key he held for the valise which should have come would not avail. It would be too large.

The same disposition which had led him to make the journey himself now impelled to test the lock without waiting to reach the privacy of his own room. After all, he was alone in the car, except for Burfoot sitting in front, and Burfoot was the man to whom the distribution would be entrusted. He drew out his bunch of keys, readily found one which would open the case, and would have done nothing to inspect its contents beyond the casual glance which he gave through the two-inch opening which followed the yielding of lock, had he not been astonished by that which the gap revealed.

With an exclamation, "What the devil's this?" he pulled the case wide open. Burfoot looked round sharply, hearing apprehension in his voice. He saw his master handling a large fragment of stone, which he held lifted half out of the case.

"Burfoot," Snacklit said, "there's some funny business here. It looks like some kind of a trap to me. We're not being followed, are we? I'm inclined to get rid of this over the Low Level Bridge."

"Followed? I'm not that sure. There's a taxi hanging on behind."

"Then double back at Sistern Road. That ought to make sure."

"Right you are, sir."

Burfoot turned the car at a left-hand street, and then turned left again, so that he was returning the way he came. After the second turn, he slowed down, so that, when Irene's taxi followed him, he was only a short distance ahead.

"So that's it?" Snacklit said. "I'll have a word with them and find out who they are, and what they think they're doing. You'd better draw up to the kerb, and if they stop, and you see me get in, just go ahead as before."

"To Snacklit House, sir?"

"Yes. You'll be all right if we don't follow, and all right if we do."

"What about Low Level Bridge, sir?"

"Not with them looking on. Give it a miss."

He got out and walked back to the taxi, which had also drawn up at the pavement a short distance behind.

He did not know what he should find—it might have been an escort sent by Professor Blinkwell for his protection—but he was surprised when he saw only a taxi driver of rather dull aspect in front, and a young, well-dressed, and attractive girl in the rear of the vehicle

Anyone less likely than she—unless it were a baby in arms—to be representing the law in pursuit of their powerful and dangerous gang would not be easy to imagine. Neither did the driver appear to be such a one as the police would have been likely to select for such a task. He thought it probable that Burfoot had made a mistake, which modified his manner, though it did not change his purpose to probe what the truth might be. He looked at the driver as he asked, "What's the game you're playing with us?"

The man, who, unlike most of his kind, was not quick at retort, did not reply. He looked round at Irene, as though implying that the question should be addressed to her.

Irene looked at a man whom she felt no occasion to fear. He was small, rather skinny in build, bald, thin-faced, with colourless eyebrows above very pale blue eyes. She looked at him closely thinking that her mission had already become more than half a success by his own act. She would be able to identify him anywhere now. And his clothes. He was well enough dressed, but that did not make him look like a gentleman. Nothing could.

Baffled by the driver's silence, he transferred his attention to her. He opened the door, and leaned in as he asked his previous question in a rather different form, "Perhaps you'll be good enough to say why you're following me?"

She smiled as she gave a flippantly evasive answer, "It must have been because you were in front."

He looked at her uncertainly, showing no appreciation of the humour of this reply. He said, "I shall need a better explanation than that."

She saw that it was useless to attempt concealment of the fact that she had been following him. After that backward turn! She said boldly, "We thought you'd got the wrong case."

He stared at her in mingled fear and bewilderment. "What made you think that?"

"Because the labels had got a bit mixed."

"And who are you?"

"I brought the case over for Mr. Kindell."

His next question was checked unspoken. Could he ask more without giving himself away to this dubious stranger? He said, "Well, you shall have your way." He went back to the front door, and got in beside the driver. As he did so, the car in front began to move ahead. He said to the driver: "You can go on following it. We don't mind."

Irene observed his action with excitement rather than apprehension. She was certainly succeeding in what Will had relied on her to do, though no one could have foreseen what was happening now. She was in a civilized city, on the side of the law, and in her own hired taxi. And the man who had got in did not appear to be a formidable kind. But she had become cautious. She decided that she would not go far in pursuit of the light grey car without having something more to say.

They had returned to their previous direction by now, the grey car leading, but at a moderate pace; certainly making no attempt to get away. The intruder sat silently beside her own driver. He had become doubtful both of the wisdom of what he had done, and of what he should do next. But what other course, he asked himself, could he have taken? A wild attempt to outdistance pursuit, perhaps ending in an accident, or the intervention of the police, with those false number plates on his car? No, it was far more prudent to take control of this young woman till he had ascertained who she was, and what peril might threaten from her. But he saw himself suddenly involved in a whirlpool of danger he did not like, and he had become correspondingly dangerous himself, in the manner of a mean, frightened, and ruthless man.

Irene, watching the route, and making mental notes of the streets they passed, had not long to debate what she should do next, for the grey car slackened speed, and turned into a wide gateway entrance, at the side of a substantial edifice, the front of which was crossed by a large sign:

SNACKLIT HOME AND HOSPITAL FOR DOMESTIC PETS

Irene spoke to the driver quickly: "Don't go in there. I've come as far as I need now."

The man slackened speed, and, as he did so, he saw a pistol in the hand of the intruder beside him. "You'll have to go on now," Snacklit said, in a voice that trembled with excitement, pushing the gun into the driver's ribs.

"Don't take any notice of him," Irene urged. "I don't suppose it's loaded, and he wouldn't dare to shoot if it were. Everyone knows you get hanged in this country if you do that. It's my taxi, not his."

"Yes, lady. But it's my life," the man answered. "I didn't bargain for this." His hands trembled on the wheel, so that the car wobbled perilously as it turned into the gateway.

Seeing that it was useless to continue protesting over that which had already occurred, she became silent, but she was intently observant now of a position which she no longer liked. She was conscious of the effort of will which was required to hold down a rising fear.

Snacklit got out of the car. "I can see," he said, "that you are a wise man. You'd better come with me and talk this over."

The man stopped his clock. He said, "I'd like to know who's going to pay my fare."

"You can't expect me to do that," Irene said. "I didn't ask you to bring me here. If you take me back where—"

"There's no hurry about that," Snacklit interposed. "But as to the fare, you'll both come with me, and we'll talk about that too."

The man appeared to be reassured by this statement, which may have seemed to him to bring the incident back to a more normal level. He got out, and Irene, seeing no advantage in sitting longer in a vehicle which there was no one to drive, did the same.

As she did this, she saw that the wide gates were already dosed. A yardman was dropping bars into their slots, while Burfoot was turning a heavy key. She disliked that, but still the taxi and its driver were with her. There was a measure of reassurance in that, which would have been more had the man been of a different sort.

Snacklit went back to the gate to give some instructions to Burfoot, which were beyond her hearing. The driver said: "I hope you know what you're doing, miss. But I wish I was out of here."

"I rather wish I were too," Irene admitted. "But you've no need to worry. Scotland Yard knows what I was doing. They'll see you right. It's that man who ought to be feeling sick."

Perhaps he should. But he gave no sign of such inward emotions as he walked back to where they were standing. He seemed to have gained confidence since he had reached his own premises, and closed his gates on the outer world.

"You'd better come in here," he said curtly, leading the way into a small office that opened out of the yard.

It contained a high desk and stool, suitable for the yard porter who usually occupied it. There was a dirty grate, with a teapot among the ashes of the fender. Beside the grate, there was an almost equally dirty chair, beyond it, an inner door.

The driver followed at once. Irene hesitated, being annoyed by the curt words, which were order rather than request. But she saw the folly of making difficulties over such points as that. She was here to hear and observe all she could.

Neither seating himself, nor inviting them to do so, Snacklit turned to the driver. "Now, my man, what was the fare?"

"There was four-and-three on the clock."

"Very well. Here's five. Now tell me who hired you, and what you know of this lady."

"I don't know nothing more than that she stopped me near Clissold Street, and told me to drive after you."

"Anyone with her?"

"Not wot I saw."

"Very well. You'd better stay here. Miss Whatever-your-name-is, you can come with me."

The man was the first to answer: "Beg pardon, sir, but I can't stay here. It's a loss of money to me."

"You needn't worry about that." Snacklit turned his attention to Irene, staring with incredulous surprise at the answer she had now given.

"I am Miss Thurlow. My father is the American Ambassador."

"Then," he asked, "what are you doing here?"

"I was forced to come here by you."

"Why were you following me before that?"

"I have told you once already."

"It didn't make sense to me."

"It was quite simple. I said—"

He interrupted: "We can't talk here. You'd better come into the house."

He opened the inner door, and led the way up a steep flight of wooden stairs. There was another door at the top, and this opened on to a well-carpeted passage. The atmosphere had suddenly changed to that of an affluent dwelling house. They passed a half-opened door of a bedroom which looked luxurious even to Irene, who had seen something of sumptuous living, and then turned into a large and very comfortable lounge.

Through a wide, single-paned window, she looked down upon a well-kept garden of surprising size for that district. The actual nature of the place was only indicated by a low, almost continuous sound of canine voices, which thick walls and carpets could not entirely deaden, and by a faint canine smell, of which those who lived there regularly had probably ceased to be aware.

On the right hand of the garden there was a high wall, from the farther side of which a stovepipe rose, sending up a column of thick black smoke, which ascended straight in a still air. What might be the meaning of that?

Snacklit's voice became smooth, and almost polite, as he said: "Now, Miss Thurlow, you'd better sit down, and tell me what the trouble is."

She remained standing as she answered: "There's no trouble that I know of. I followed you because there'd been a mistake about the case you had from Mrs. Collinson. The right one was delivered there just after you left."

He stared at this, which had implications he could not accept or reject. Was it possible that she was one of themselves? Or an innocent blunderer, who might do no harm if he should say or do nothing foolish to her? It would have seemed more probable but for the piece of stone in the case he had been given. That *must* have been put in to delude him with the expected weight. But was even that certain? Might it not have been put up to mislead someone else?— someone of the Customs, or the police? And by some fluke, it had been given to him? And this was nothing more than an attempt to put matters right? If so, he had come near to being an utter fool. Might, indeed, be said to have come more than near by the way he had treated the taxi driver, which would be hard to explain. Yet a ten-pound note will do much. The man did not appear to be of an aggressive temper. But he must not think. He must *know*. What he said was, "You didn't seem in any hurry to catch me up."

"The man was a slow driver; and you've got a much better car."

He gave no sign that he saw the weakness of that reply. He changed the subject, "You say your father's the American Ambassador?"

"Yes, he is."

"Then you ought not to be wandering about alone here. I think I ought to phone the police, for your own protection."

"Thank you, but I am quite capable of looking after myself. I shall be all right when I leave here."

"Perhaps you're not the best judge of that."

He went out as he spoke. He did not close the door, and she wondered whether it would be worthwhile to attempt to escape to the security of the open street. But she judged correctly that it would not be easy to do. And if he were really phoning the police—but she did not believe that.

Well, while she must remain here, there was no reason she should not take the comfort that the room provided. She sank into the depths of a padded chair.

She sat there a long time, her mind reviewing and memorizing what had occurred, and reaching the sound conclusion that her presence in that house provided a difficult problem for its owner to solve. With less certain logic, she offered herself the comfortable deduction that she had nothing about which to worry. That was for the proprietor of the Snacklit Home. And so, relaxation from past excitement, comfort, and warmth had their natural effect, and when, a full hour afterwards, the door opened quietly, she was so nearly asleep that she was unaware of what was happening until it was almost too late to speak.

She looked up to see a tea tray on a low table beside her, and a maid servant retiring through the door. She called sharply and rather incoherently, on which the girl came a step back into the room.

"How long have I—what time is it?" she began, as she rose from the chair. "Will you tell Mr.—the gentleman—that I cannot stay longer? I should like a taxi called. That is, if mine—"

She saw the uselessness of saying more to a girl whose vacuous expression did not change. She knew the event could not end in that casual manner. Not, at least, owing to any demand by her. Not unless he whom she had so inaccurately described a moment before should have decided that there was no more that could be usefully said, and that it would be prudent to let her go without the opportunity for further words.

The girl said tonelessly: "Yes, madam. I'll let the master know what you say."

She withdrew, and Irene became conscious of healthy appetite as she gazed at the well-laden tray which had been placed beside her.

Being detained in so outrageous a manner, she felt that she need feel no scruple in accepting anything which might be provided, though it were from an enemy's hand. The question of hospitality did not arise. But another did. Most inopportunely, she remembered that she was dealing with those who trafficked in poisonous or otherwise overpowering drugs. Suppose that the teapot, towards which her hand was stretched, should contain some subtle tasteless drug which might destroy memory, or break down the power of the will, or produce unconsciousness, during which she might be subject to any outrage, or removed to she knew not where. Suppose she should become a slobbering lunatic in the next hour?

There are possibilities when the chemist works without scruple or fear of law which are literally worse than death.

But she had a healthy and sanguine mind, it was already past the time at which she was used to taking a more substantial meal, and the call of hunger prevailed. She told herself, with some reason, that, even were it intended that the worst possible fate should be hers, there was a probability that she would be questioned first. They must be puzzled by the course of events, and would seek to obtain information from her. The stones in the suitcase would be hard for any theory to fit. The really puzzling thing was that Snacklit did not return. She would eat that which had been provided, and then, if she were still alone, she would endeavour to leave the house. She could detect no strange taste in the tea. The muffins were good. And so was the strawberry jam.

CHAPTER XXIX.

MR. SNACKLIT THINKS

THERE WERE GOOD reasons why Snacklit left Irene alone for an hour, or more nearly two. He had a deadly fear that he had blundered into the observation of the law in a way which, whatever he might do now, would still be fatal to him—or, as an almost equal fear, that he had interfered with plans which might otherwise have gone smoothly in a way which Professor Blinkwell would not forgive. Whatever the truth might be, it was imperative that he should know where his danger lay.

To do this in the permitted manner, it was necessary to get the preliminary message, which the Professor received while at dinner, transmitted to his butler through three intermediaries, then to wait for the five minutes which were allowed for the return by the same circuitous method of the information that he had received it, and then to converse with him under assumed names, using a code adapted for such contingencies and from a different call box from that which he had previously used.

And, after this, he was in no mood for an instant interview with the young woman he had so rashly entrapped. He required time to think. He was undecided, frightened, and rendered abnormally dangerous by his fear.

The form of his conversation with Professor Blinkwell would have rendered it difficult for him to learn all the facts of the case even had the Professor been willing to give them. But he had been able, in oblique words, to explain sufficiently to enable him, with his superior knowledge, to understand more completely, and that gentleman had made two things clear. First, that he regarded Snacklit's action as being foolish to the verge of imbecility, and as having hazarded the security of the gang to a degree that would be difficult to forgive. And second, that he must get out of the mess in his own way, and without assistance or further contacts with those whose security he had already jeopardized.

He was to deal with those who were now in his power in his own way. That might mean anything. But, in fact, it meant one thing only. *In his own way.* Professor Blinkwell and he both knew what that way was. When he said it, the Professor had pronounced sentences of death both on the taxi driver and the ambassador's daughter. As to the first, Snacklit saw that it might be best. He had thought of bribery, but that held a risk. The man might refuse the offered notes. He might accept them and still report the whole incident to the police. He knew that Professor Blinkwell did not approve of risks. He made it a rule not to incur them. Here was illustration of that. He had suggested—it might be said ordered—the two murders, and what was there that could be urged against him, even though every word should have been recorded. He had said that Snacklit must deal with his trouble in his own way. Who could blame him for that?

Snacklit observed this without resentment, for he knew that Professor Blinkwell urged the same elaborate cautions on others which he practised himself. The drastic action which he now directed was (he would have said) the path of safety now.

And as to the man, Snacklit agreed. Indeed, the return of the taxi to the Holborn cab rank, which was the one thing which had been done instantly, as the Professor had advised, was a preliminary to the action against him that the occasion required. That could be no cause for worry. Enquiry (if there should be any, which would depend upon the existence of near relatives and their dispositions) would be moderate at most, and that he would ever be traced to Snacklit House was an extreme improbability. Even if he were, against the blank denials which would be given, what proof would there be?

That was, if the girl should be silenced. Professor Blinkwell had seen that at once. Pondering the problem with slower brains, though he was far from a dull man, Snacklit saw it also.

To destroy the girl would rouse a far louder outcry than would follow the disappearance of any taxi driver in London. Taxi drivers are a numerous race. Ambassadors' daughters are rare, and correspondingly valuable. Yet to destroy the driver and let her live might be most dangerous of all.

He regretted now that he had led her to his own home. He should have driven in any other direction rather than that. So he saw now. But he had not known who she was till it was too late. He felt that she should have warned him earlier. The treatment he had received was unfair. Being stirred to indignation by the view of the course of events, he felt a lively hatred of its author, which assisted his resolution to deal with her in a way which would remove the fear of her ever standing in the witness box to testify against him.

It might seem to superficial consideration to be a perilous course, but actually it was the one in which safety lay. Yet precipitate action—? No. He remembered a counsel of priceless wisdom he had once been privileged to hear from Professor Blinkwell's lips. A valid though subtle distinction had been drawn between the course adopted, in which boldness might often reduce risk, and the method of execution, in which caution must be the unvarying rule. The Professor had argued, with illuminating illustrations, that this rule is often reversed, by which peril and failure come. Many who are cautious in the design are careless in the detail of what they do. At this point in his reflections he touched the bell. He said: "Take the young lady some tea."

CHAPTER XXX.

A SKIRMISH OF DEADLY WORDS

PROFESSOR BLINKWELL sat in the lounge with his wife and niece. He was engaged upon the study of a chemical formula of some complexity, which had been sent to him by a brother scientist who was anxious to obtain the benefit of his opinion upon an unexpected difficulty which he had encountered in the course of experimental work. A radio programme of light music was occupying the attention of the ladies sufficiently to secure their contented silence and allow the concentration that the subject required. If his thoughts strayed to the dangerous imbecility of Mr. Snacklit, and its probable consequences, he gave no sign of such deviation. And, indeed, there may have been none, for. Professor Blinkwell had the exceptional quality of mind which will make reality of its own pretence. He had decided that an attitude of utter aloofness to the criminalities which, his intelligence told him, would be the natural result of the orders he had issued was the right one to adopt for his own security. He dismissed them forthwith from his mind. They were matters in which he had no part. Of which he had no knowledge. Which could have no approval from him.

A maid-servant was at the door. "If you please, sir, Mr. Kindell has called, and would like to see you "

"Kindell, Rachel? Oh, yes. I will see the young man."

As the girl withdrew, he rose and switched off the radio.

"Ruth," he said to his wife, who was already preparing to leave the room, "I don't think you'll want to stay. Nor you, Myra." He waited for the moment that must pass before his wife left, and continued: "This is an occasion on which discretion of speech is imperative. Extreme discretion. You had better leave it entirely to me."

Myra rose also, though with less readiness than her aunt, who, besides that she was a professional invalid, which is an exacting occupation, always made it clear that she took no interest in her husband's business affairs. But Myra had no doubt of her own capacity to avoid indiscretions of speech, and would have been interested to hear a conversation which her uncle, she did not doubt, would be able to lead in his own way. Curiosity urged her to remain.

But there was no time to argue, and the idea of refusing obedience did not enter her mind. Rather sulkily she withdrew and Professor Blinkwell was alone when Kindell entered the room.

The Professor led the conversation at once. He grasped his visitor's hand with his maximum of cordiality as he said suavely: "This is an unexpected pleasure. I must congratulate you upon having convinced the Sûreté that you were not involved in that dreadful crime—as it is easy to see that you must have done, or you would not be in London now."

In the brief period which he had had for reflection as he had been driven from Scotland Yard to the Professor's door, Kindell had decided that the time for caution had gone. He did not know in what peril Irene might be, nor how great might be the importance of time. But the doubt was enough to justify almost any violence or any trick which would release her from what he felt must be, at best, some form of detention against her will. He knew that he was dealing with ruthless and frightened men—men who would think only of their own security, and would be ready to buy it at any cost. They must be attacked now, without a moment's delay, and without reservation of any weapon he had.

Yet when the Professor met him with a pose of amity, he saw that it might be best to let him show his hand somewhat further before exposing his own. He said, "Even when they are less than satisfied, they cannot go far without proof."

"Under the French system of judicial enquiry," the Professor answered, "I should have said that they can go quite a long way." His voice had a faint note of distaste, as though he disapproved of a system of justice inferior to that of his native land, as an Englishman would be likely to do. He added: "I should not have expected that you would be so promptly released unless their suspicions have found another object. Did you hear anything to suggest that they have solved the mystery of who the murderer could have been?"

"I heard a rumour that they had become interested in the movements of one of the waiters at the hotel."

Professor Blinkwell looked mildly interested. "Yes," he said doubtfully, "it is a possible idea. Yet what motive could he have had? Perhaps homicidal mania should be considered. There are cases of epilepsy which have had such unhappy results."

137

Kindell felt that he was gaining nothing by these exchanges. He became delusively frank in his reply: "I doubt whether epilepsy would be a sufficient explanation. There is another matter in which the man has acted in a way which may admit of innocent explanation, but it is hard to guess what it can be."

"Indeed? Then he is presumably under arrest, which will explain the promptness of your release?"

"That is more than I can say. But the matter which I was about to explain did not come to my knowledge until I had returned to London. He used my name in an audacious manner, evidently thinking that I should be detained in Paris for a longer time than I was."

"Whereas—if I may make a probable guess, and it should be a matter which may be admitted in—shall I say in friendly confidence?—you were actually in no danger at all, being in the confidence of our own police?"

Kindell met this direct and most unexpected attack with a smile which showed him to be equal to his opponent's craft. "What," he asked in a noncommittal tone, "should make you think that?"

"It was Myra's idea rather than mine. It was something she overheard—the inevitable chatter of the hotel—which gave it to her—but it has some support in the fact that you are in London now."

"And they arrested me as a sign of their friendly regard? I should have preferred that they had shown it in other ways. But perhaps Myra was also able to explain why they did that?"

"If she was, she did not confide to me. But now you are with us again you can explain it all. That is, if you would like to look in tomorrow at an earlier hour. She has retired tonight, having one of those headaches which will occur when she has nothing more urgent upon her mind."

"I am afraid tomorrow might be too late."

"Too late? My suggestion was that you should make an earlier call."

"So I understood. You have politely asked me to go. But I came to ask your immediate help."

"Then why not have said so at once? If it be within reason and within my power it is not likely to be refused."

Professor Blinkwell said this in a tone of friendly rebuke, and Kindell felt that it was time for a retort which it would be less easy to turn aside.

"It is your influence with Mrs. Collinson that I am anxious to have."

But there was no evidence that the shot went home. "She is a lady whom you think I could influence? Perhaps you will say why, and what you would ask me to do. It is not a name which I can recollect as that of one whom I know."

"Myra knows her."

"That is a different matter. Myra's female friends are more than I am ever likely to count. It may be a reason why you should ask for her assistance rather than mine in whatever entanglement—unless," he added, with a sudden change of tone, as of one whose mind was illuminated by a new idea, "it is such a matter as you would prefer that she should not know?"

Kindell saw that he was making no progress of any kind. The Professor's skill in verbal fence was impregnable against attempted surprise. He said: "I had better tell you plainly what has occurred."

The Professor rose. "Kindell," he said, "I don't want to be rude. But if you really want me to do you a favour, you are scarcely going about it in the best way. I was engaged upon important and urgent work when you were announced, in spite of which I did not refuse to see you, but I have given you more than one hint already that I am anxious to resume it without further delay. If you like to come to dinner tomorrow—I shall be fully engaged during the day—I will listen to whatever troubles you have, but I must ask you to be good enough to go now."

"Then I must be equally plain. I am engaged on a matter that will not wait. We have lost too much time already in talk that has led us nowhere. I am concerned for Miss Thurlow's safety, and if you will assist me in that matter, it may be beneficial in other ways."

"Miss Thurlow? You mean the charming daughter of the American Ambassador? Myra pointed her out to me as one who was friendly to you. But what could threaten her safety in a country where we might say that she is an international guest?"

"She disappeared this evening, and the driver of her taxi is missing also."

"Then I can understand your anxiety, but I can assure you that she has not eloped with me. It is not a matter in which I could assist you at all."

"But I think you could. Superintendent Allenby is of the same opinion."

"I cannot imagine how. And I think you will be wasting your time, as you are certainly wasting mine. But I will hear what you have to say."

"Then it is soon said. The French waiter, Gustav, took a valise to Miss Thurlow, which he asked her to get through the Customs with her father's luggage. He said it was mine, and that the request was a message from me, which was a lie. He gave her a label to put on it, so that on its arrival in England it could be forwarded, as he said, to me. The label was addressed to Mrs. Collinson's house, of which I knew nothing. By a very natural error, it was put on the wrong case. When the mistake was discovered, after it had been delivered, Miss Thurlow took the right case to Mrs. Collinson's. She was just too late to prevent the man for whom it must have been really meant driving away with it. She followed him to correct the error. That was several hours ago, and she has not returned."

"There may be one of a dozen simple explanations of that."

"The taxi which she hired has been found on a cab rank, but the driver was not there."

"Having, perhaps, gone for a drink?"

"His absence was far too long for such an explanation."

"It is certainly a queer tale. But if the police have it in hand, it is hard to see what more you can do."

"It was the police who suggested I should come to you."

"But why, in the name of common sense, should they do that?"

"Because they thought you would have influence with Mrs. Collinson to persuade her to give the address of the man to whom the suitcase belongs."

"You mean that she has refused this information to them?"

"I cannot say that. They may not have tried."

"I must say again that it is a queer tale. And that I have any influence with the lady must, I fear, be imagination rather than fact. But it may be a matter on which two will do better than one. If you are set upon going to see her now, I will not decline to come with you and add my persuasions to yours. But on what you tell me, it is a matter that the police should not be leaving to us. Have you a car waiting? Then we will go in. that. It will be slightly more expeditious than ordering mine. If you will excuse me for a moment, I will be with you."

"May I use your phone?"

"By all means. The police should know what we are proposing to do."

Waving his hand to the instrument, the Professor left the room. He was back almost immediately, having put on his hat and coat, and given some brief instructions to his butler, which would result in further devious telephone communications after they had left the house.

Meanwhile, Kindell had telephoned to Superintendent Allenby, and learned that there was still no news of Irene or her driver. He said that he had explained the position frankly to Professor Blink-well, who would go with him to Mrs. Collinson's He would not say more, fearing that he might be overheard. But he would have liked to add that his frankness had had one important omission. He had intended to lead the Professor to hope, perhaps to believe, that the nature of the contents of the valise was not known—perhaps was not even suspected—by the police, and that there had been a genuine error in regard to its labelling. Had he been successful in that? It was hard to guess.

CHAPTER XXXI.

MRS. COLLINSON HOLDS HER OWN

PROFESSOR BLINKWELL and Kindell entered the waiting taxi together, each feeling that he had been victor in the verbal skirmish from which they came.

Kindell felt that there was evidence of success in the mere fact that the Professor, with whatever protests of ignorance, had consented to accompany him. He had a sanguine hope that, however cunningly it might be cloaked, the Professor's real purpose was to assure himself of Irene's safety, and arrange for her release from whatever detention she might be experiencing.

On his side, Professor Blinkwell, with greater subtlety, saw that he had been invited to do what he wished, but would otherwise have considered too dangerous. He felt that he was acting in a natural manner, and as an innocent man, impelled by friendly feeling, would be likely to do.

Mrs. Collinson would be warned before his arrival that he was a stranger to her. Apart from that, she could not give much away, even though she were subject to persuasion or threats, for on the matter which Kindell was investigating there was very little she knew.

They were admitted at once, though the hour was becoming late. Becky showed them into an empty room, and asked for their names. She returned immediately to say that her mistress would be with them in a few minutes.

Five minutes later the lady entered the room. Her fingers were on a blouse button, which she fastened as she appeared. Without mentioning the matter at all, she implied that the visit had surprised her when she had been preparing for rest.

"Mr. Kindell?" she asked tentatively, looking at the Professor as she spoke.

He corrected her error, introducing himself and his companion. He added: "Mr. Kindell is concerned about a muddle which has occurred, and a young lady he believes to be lost. He will explain it better than I should be able to do."

Mrs. Collinson looked at Kindell as though he were an enigma she could neither understand nor approve.

"This," she asked, "is really Mr. Kindell? Then I should be glad if he would explain what has occurred, and the use which he has made of this house. You may not know that he was here a few hours ago, and then spoke of himself as though he were another man. He was a messenger from the American Embassy. Or at least that was what he said then."

Kindell was quick to answer that which had not been addressed to him: "That was what I was. But I wished to see whether you knew me, in view of the use which had been made of my name here."

"Then I can tell you at once that I never heard as much as your name till I got the postcard to say that you were sending something here which your friend would collect, and, if there had been any address upon it I should have written to say that it was a liberty which I could not permit."

"Might I see that postcard?"

"You could with pleasure if it had not been destroyed. It lay about for a day or so, and then I put it on the fire. Actually, I thought it had been wrongly addressed to me."

"Then you might have given it back to the postman."

"I thought of that. But what use would it have been? It had no address on it except mine, and that was correct."

She lied readily, having thought out this explanation beforehand. Professor Blinkwell, listening in admiration, thought that he had underestimated her capacities for duplicity. Perhaps he might have made greater use of her in the past than he had thought wise to do!

Kindell did not know how much to believe, by which her effort of imagination may be classified as a success. He was not fully convinced, for the presence of Myra at the house was a certain fact, by which others must be assessed. But he was uncertain how much Mrs. Collinson might have been accomplice or merely tool.

As the latter, she might know less, but what she did know she should be the more ready to tell. As he considered this, he had a doubt of whether Professor Blinkwell's presence was to be the advantage which he had hoped. But none of these reflections could change the direction of his attack.

"What we want to know now," he said, "is, in particular, the name and address of the man to whom the wrong case was delivered."

"It wasn't delivered anywhere. Your man came and took it away."

"That was what I meant. But he wasn't my man at all. It's his name and address that I am anxious to know."

"But that doesn't sound sense. You must have arranged for him to call."

"I know nothing about it. The case was not mine, nor was it sent by me. My name was used without my authority or knowledge."

Mrs. Collinson had the look of one who accepts a surprising fact, and is endeavouring to adjust her mind to its implications.

"I wonder," she said, "why anyone should have done that. But it's quite natural that you feel annoyed."

"Mr. Kindell," Professor Blinkwell interposed, "is more than annoyed. There is a young lady involved in the matter who cannot be found, and he is anxious to trace her without delay."

"Then I'm sorry," the lady replied, "but I can't do much to help you. All I know is that someone came in a car and said he was from Mr. Kindell and took the case—the first one—away. I didn't see him myself."

"But your maid must have seen him," the Professor insisted "Will you permit us to question her?"

Mrs. Collinson's reply was to touch the bell. When the girl appeared, she said, "Becky, I want you to tell these gentlemen all you can remember about the man who called for the case."

"I didn't notice him that particular. He was quite a nice gentleman."

Kindell asked, "I suppose you'd know him if you should see him again."

"Oh, yes, sir. I think I should."

"Can you describe him?"

The girl appeared to make a genuine effort of memory. She said he was dark. But not so very. Short. But not that short. She thought he had been wearing a grey suit. It all amounted to nothing. Both the Professor and Mrs. Collinson appeared to be anxious to persuade her to talk, and to stimulate her memory. But Kindell saw that it was a useless pursuit. His real anxiety had become to decide whether he were being elaborately fooled.

But even if that were so, it did not follow that it was not the Professor's purpose to lead to Irene's recovery—perhaps by such a method as should place him under an obligation he could not easily decline to admit.

Yet, be that as it might, it appeared evident that they were to have little assistance from either of the women who were now before them. Either they were telling all that they knew, or the Professor's influence (if he had any) was not being exerted in the right way.

The idea came to him (in which he was wrong) that as Gustav had provided the label giving Mrs. Collinson's address, he might also know that to which the case was being taken away. And it was with the intention of reminding the Professor of the danger which (as he rightly hoped) might lie in any confession the French waiter could be persuaded to make that he said aloud: "There's one chance yet. We don't know what the French police may be getting from Gustav now."

"Yes," Professor Blinkwell agreed readily, "their methods may be getting quite a lot from him, if I remember the sort he was. The trouble would be to know what to believe."

To himself, Kindell admitted the force of that argument. The man who had professed to be his own messenger to Irene, and had given her the valise in his name, would not be likely to be short of a useful lie.

"Yes," he said, "there's always that difficulty."

"Perhaps," the Professor suggested, "they'd have a better prospect of getting him to say what you want to know if he were not afraid that it might be used against him in connection with the policeman's murder."

"I daresay they would."

"I suppose the police here are a good deal more concerned about the American girl."

It was a statement rather than a question, but Kindell had become sufficiently familiar with the subtlety of the Professor's conversational methods to accept it differently. He regarded it as a leading question. Or rather, as an indication of the lines on which a business deal might be arranged. "Than about Reynard's murder, you mean? I should say they are. That's a headache for Paris rather than Scotland Yard. But they'll naturally be anxious that Miss Thurlow should not get into any trouble here."

"There may be the offer of a reward, if the young lady should not be promptly found?"

"I should think there will. But I hope we shall have her back before there's time to advertise that."

"May I suggest that an assurance that whoever may be holding her now will not be required to explain the reason for her detention—if a channel for such communication could be discovered— might be of material assistance? That is, if she really be detained against her own will, as you seem disposed—perhaps too readily—to assume?"

"Yes. Perhaps it would. But it would be a difficult undertaking to give."

"By the police, yes. But if you could make such a bargain yourself, into which they might not intrude, I should suppose, if the safety of the daughter of the American Ambassador should be involved, it is a case where they might be willing to close their eyes?"

"You think her safety is really at stake?"

"I can only infer from what I have heard from you—but it is for you to judge rather than me."

Kindell hesitated how to reply. His own inclination was to place Irene's safety before any other consideration, and—she being who she was—he saw that the police might take the same view. But he saw also that it would be an exceedingly difficult bargain to define, and one which he had no authority to make. Even a personal promise, such as a private citizen might feel free to give, was a dereliction of duty by him unless he had permission for what he did. What, he wondered, would the consequence be, if he should not bargain, but threaten? If he should challenge these treacherous criminals by an assertion that the police were already aware of their nefarious activities, and that their positions, perilous already, would be tenfold worse if they should not aid him in securing her safe return from wherever—as he would protest—they must know her to be?

But if he should take this course, and be confronted only by indignation and denial? What should he do then? Was it not better to accept Professor Blinkwell's suggestion, and endeavour to come to terms in a more delicate way?

The girl interrupted the moment's silence which his hesitation involved. She had been standing uncertainly at the door, neither having been required to stay nor given permission to go. "Is there anything more, ma'am?" she asked.

Her question reminded Kindell of one thing that he had not asked, because he knew it already, but he saw that her reply might be an indication of how far he should believe her on other points. He said: "Just a moment, Becky. Can you tell me what kind of car the man came in?"

"Do you mean the first man, sir, or the second?"

"I don't understand you. You didn't say there were two."

"There was the man who fetched the second case."

"How long ago was that?"

"About an hour ago, sir. Perhaps a bit less."

"What sort of a man was he?"

"He was rather thin, sir. I didn't look at him particularly. He seemed in a hurry."

"You didn't tell me about this, Becky," her mistress said, with a faint note of rebuke in her voice.

"No, ma'am. I didn't know that I need."

Professor Blinkwell asked, "Did he return the first case when he took the other away?"

"No, sir. He said that would be sent back in the morning."

"And what sort of car did he have?" Kindell went on.

"It looked like a taxi, sir. I feel sure that's what it was."

It all sounded plausible enough. If they were all acting, it was being cleverly done. Yet he was far from sure. But he saw one thing he did not like. Only Irene had known that he was returning to the house with the second case.

The man in the grey car might have opened the first one and seen the nature of its contents. But that would give him no reason to expect that the second would be subsequently delivered with its contents intact. The natural inference would be very different from that.

Either these people were giving him concocted lies, or Irene must herself have supplied the information which had caused the second man to come, and that implied that she had been in contact—in conversation—either voluntary or otherwise—with the man she had been pursuing. That was not what she had agreed to do. She was to have followed only. It did no more than confirm what he had already supposed. But it was an unwelcome confirmation, and, in view of the way in which her taxi had been returned to the rank, it had a most sinister sound. He resumed his interrupted conversation with Professor Blinkwell by saying "Yes, I suppose you're right, that I'm the one to judge; but, all the same, I should be glad to know what you think."

Professor Blinkwell's tone was considerate as he replied: "I don't want to be an alarmist, and I should be very sorry to say anything that would make you additionally anxious. But from the facts you have given me, I do think that it would be prudent to endeavour to get in touch with the parties concerned, and make the best bargain you can for the young lady's release."

"You think that could be done?"

"I think it ought to be tried. I would indeed make an effort for you myself—I could not, of course, undertake that it would succeed—but I might have to pledge my word that there would be no subsequent punitive action of any kind. You would have to go back to Scotland Yard and telephone me an explicit authority to that effect."

"Very well, I'll see what I can do."

"Then you had better have the taxi in which we came, as time is important to you. I will get another, and shall be back at my own house by when you will be getting through to me."

The Professor looked as though he had something further to say, but Kindell was through the door without waiting to hear.

When he had gone and Becky had left the room, the Professor said: "I can see that you have a reliable maid. And your own attitude was exactly that which the position required. I shall not forget."

He shook hands with Mrs. Collinson with more than his usual amiability, but when he was alone in the taxi which he had hailed for his own use, his jaw was hard set and there was black anger and ruthless cruelty in his eyes.

"The fool," he thought. "The damned fool. To land me in this!" As to Snacklit, he had no doubt at all. His days must be nearly done. But as to Irene, even if the police should be willing to make such a bargain as he had proposed, he was not sure that it would be wise to carry it out. He was clear of complicity now. Clear of anything that could be proved. Dead men tell no tales. And it is the same with girls. The question needed most careful thought.

CHAPTER XXXII.

IRENE HAS SEEN TOO MUCH

IRENE HAD CLEARED the tea tray. Any anxiety she may have felt had left her appetite unsubdued. She brushed a crumb from her dress. She stood up. She was inclined to walk out, or to find what the obstruction would be.

Then she had an idea at which she paused. Was it not possible that they had sent for the valise which she had said had been delivered to Mrs. Collinson, and that they were only waiting to see that it was intact before releasing her, with the admission that all was well?

The tea, from which she was feeling no ill-effects, seemed to support that comfortable theory. And, if it were so, would it not be an undignified folly to make a fuss, and perhaps have an unpleasant altercation, for which a little patience would show that there had been no need?

It was a correct theory so far as that Snacklit's recollections of the Professor's advice had caused him to send a discreet and indirect messenger for the valise, and it was true that he had decided to reserve the question of how he should dispose of her until he should know that that had been done, and, as he hoped, all possibilities of other complications removed. It was too sanguine only in its assumption that, if the valise were found to have its lock intact and its contents undisturbed, there would be immediate freedom for her.

But hesitating over this possibility, she walked over to the window and looked down on to the garden. It was still solitary. Its high walls were such that she saw it could not be overlooked. If she should endeavour to reach it, would it provide an easier exit than she might find through the front premises? She saw nothing to encourage that hope. Solid wooden doors in the walls...almost certainly locked. But someone—something—was coming under the window now. Coming from the direction of the yard into which she had been driven. It was a hand-truck being wheeled by two men. They crossed the broad path beneath the window to a door in the wall on the further side—the wall over which the chimney showed from which the thick black smoke rose, as she had seen it an hour before.

There was a large rug cast over that with which the truck was loaded. As the men put the truck down, and one pushed past it to unlock the door, the rug fell somewhat aside. It was adjusted almost at once, but what she had seen was beyond doubt: two booted feet, and a man's leg.

The door opened. The truck was through. The door closed. From the chimney over the wall the smoke rose.

Irene did not know that the blood had left her face, though she felt her heart beat so hard that she might have thought that it could be heard by anyone in the room. She looked round and Snacklit was at her side. He must have seen what she had seen. Must have seen that she had seen it. He must have seen her fear. And now she was going to faint.

"Miss Thurlow," she heard, "you had better sit down. There are one or two things I should like to ask you."

She did not faint. With a supreme effort of will she controlled her fear. As she sat down, each heartbeat was less than the one before. She looked straight at a man whose eyes did not meet hers as she answered: "Yes. What is it you want to know?"

CHAPTER XXXIII.

A Question of Red Hair

MR. SNACKLIT IGNORED the garden incident and its effect upon her, which he could not have failed to observe. He said, "Miss Thurlow, you will be interested to hear that the right case has now been collected, and that incident may be considered closed. What I want to know is what your part in the matter has been."

"I have told you that already. What I want to know is why you have kept me here, which you must know that you have no right to do."

"Considering how you followed me, and how you made an excuse which it was impossible to believe, you can hardly complain if I wished to check your statement on the one point on which it was capable of confirmation, before deciding whether you should be handed over to the police. You must remember that I've only your own word—which I have no reason to trust—that you are Miss Thurlow at all."

"Well, you've had your confirmation now, so there's no more to be said."

"On the contrary, there is a great deal. If you will give me a full and convincing account of what your connection with this matter has been, and at whose suggestion you were following me in the way you did, it may be important for you."

"I'm not going over it all again, if you mean that."

"Then you will be a very foolish young woman."

"I'll tell you one thing. The police know where I am. They may be here any minute now."

"I see no reason to believe that."

"Well, it's true, anyway. They have the number of your car." It was an unfortunate attempt to impress by particularity. The man's eyes were derisively contemptuous as he replied: "Very well. They've got the number of the car. Now, while they're on the way

151

here perhaps you'll tell me why you were following it in the way you did."

She did not attempt to repeat her previous evasion that his car had been the faster vehicle. She said boldly, "I did it to find out where you were taking the wrong case."

"And why were you doing that?"

"Mr. Kindell asked me to, while he took the right one to the house."

"And who may he be?"

"He's something to do with the police."

"That's what you meant when you said the police had got the number of my car?"

"Yes, it's true. And they won't be long in finding their way here. You may be sure of that."

Her answers had been intended to alarm him in such a way as would be likely to conduce to her own safety, for she had become in deadly fear since she had looked out of the window—a fear made more acute by the belief that Snacklit knew now much she had seen.

She was partially successful. The man became silent, mentally weighing the implications of what he did not doubt to have been truly spoken. He did not like it. He hated mention of the police. So far, however numerous his crimes may have been, he had never been even questioned, never suspected at all. That must be his greatest asset now. The police would not be likely to turn their eyes in his direction. If they were invited to do so by others, they would soon be satisfied and turn them away. That was, if this girl did not exist. She had become a mortal danger to him. Only her destruction— literal destruction of every bone in her body—could bring safety to him.

As to the car—she did not know that the number it had borne belonged to another of the same kind. (Neither did he know of the promptness of the police discovery that that car *could* not be the one that had been used by him.) But he saw clearly that the time for circumspection had gone. If suspicions sooner or later were to be directed upon him, the essential matter was that all manner of evidence should be swept away. And at once. The girl who had brought Irene's tea was at the door again, "If you please, sir, you're wanted on the telephone, most particular."

"Any name?"

"It's something about a terrier with a bad ear."

Snacklit rose at once. That was a code phrase which was never used except to convey a message from Professor Blinkwell himself, and of an exceptional urgency.

"Kate," he said, "I shall only be away for a few minutes. You must stay here till I come back. Meanwhile, this young lady will remain. If she should attempt to leave the room, you will call Billson at once."

He hurried out.

She looked at the girl. A hard face, though comely with youth and health. It was her one chance. Good or bad, she must try. And there was no time for a slow approach. She said, "You can't all be murderers here."

The girl seemed to be startled for a moment, and then controlled herself, and looked at Irene with curiosity.

"Murderers?" she echoed. "I don't know what you mean. It's a dogs' home. They kill lots of them."

"And taxi drivers?"

"Taxi drivers?" the girl repeated. She stared in what appeared to be genuine bewilderment.

"Anyway, they killed one in the last hour. I saw them wheel his body across the garden and take it through the door below."

"That would be from the yard. It sounds silly. They couldn't have put him to sleep there."

"I didn't say they did. They might have killed him some other way."

"I expect he was just drunk."

"And covered up, head and all, with a great rug? I tell you he was a dead man."

"Well, anyway, it's no business of ours."

"It's very much my business. He was the man who drove me here. I'll give you fifty pounds if you'll get me out before he comes back."

"I shouldn't think it worthwhile. I should get sacked more likely than not. I've got a good job here."

"Suppose I say eighty?"

"I can see it first?"

"I haven't got it here. If you come with me to Grosvenor Gardens I'll give it to you at once."

"We couldn't get away without being seen. And after that, money wouldn't be much use to me."

"Isn't it worth trying?"

The girl stared at her with expressionless eyes. It was impossible to tell what she thought. Irene controlled herself to silence till she should hear her reply. Till she had it, she felt it hard to guess what further argument would avail.

"You're sure they killed him?" the girl asked at last.

"He was alive when he drove me here."

"I daresay they did. They kill beautiful dogs. Mr. Snacklit likes doing that."

"We're losing time. If we're going—"

"It's not that simple, Miss. There's Billson too—was Billson one of them two?"

"I don't know who Billson is."

"Did one of them have red hair?"

"I didn't notice; but I don't think so."

"I'd like to hear what he says."

The girl went to the door and gave a shrill whistle. A moment later a man came into the room, showing a close-cropped head of red hair and a sharp-nosed, foxy face.

"Bill" the girl said, with a familiarity which was equally evident in his manner to her, "this lady says a taxi driver's been killed in the yard, and they've just burnt his body. I've told her that, if they did, it was nothing to do with you."

The man did not appear to regard this statement as incredible, but, unless he were an exceptionally good actor, it was a surprising item of news.

"I hadn't heard tell of that," he said. "The master told me to stay by the stairs, and not let anyone go down unless he came along with them."

"This young lady says she'll give me eighty pounds if I'll let her out.

"Or a hundred," Irene interrupted quickly, "if you're sharing between you."

The man looked at her sharply. "You'd like to get out," he asked, "to make trouble for us? That'll have to be what the master says."

"There's plenty of trouble coming," Irene replied, "whether I get out or not. But I shouldn't make any for you. I might save your life."

"I'd like to know how you'd do that."

"By saying that I saw the two men who'd got the taxi driver's body, and that neither of them had red hair."

"I don't know that anyone's been killed. It sounds just a tale to me."

"Well; it isn't. You'll find somebody's going to get hanged. More than one, I expect. But I don't want anyone to get hanged for murdering me."

The man looked at her speculatively. It had become obvious that he believed her tale, and was considering whether it would be best for himself that he should remain loyal to his employer or purchase the immunity she had offered at the price of assisting her to escape.

But as he hesitated Snacklit re-entered the room.

CHAPTER XXXIV.

MR. THURLOW DECLINES TO WAIT

KINDELL RETURNED TO Scotland Yard to find Superintendent Allenby still sitting at his desk and Mr. Thurlow pacing restlessly across the room. It was as though he had left them for a moment only, but Mr. Thurlow showed how different it had seemed to him by the impatient exclamation: "What a time you've been! And all the while the superintendent here begging me to do nothing, and another hour nearly gone, and Irene—it doesn't bear thinking of what may be happening to her! I can only hope you've done something now!"

"I have a proposal from Professor Blinkwell. He might arrange for her return if he were assured that there would be no unpleasant consequences to follow."

There was satisfaction in the superintendent's eyes, as well as surprise, as he exclaimed: "You really got him to say that! It's the best day's work you've done yet."

"Of course, he didn't put it into those words. He's as slippery as an eel. He said if he were to negotiate, he would need authority to make terms of that kind."

"Did he say about what? If it were only about the girl's abduction—if that's what's happened—and she were safely returned, we might possibly—I suppose he didn't say anything about drug-smuggling?"

"No. He did mention the Paris murder."

"Did he? That's interesting. It's very near to an admission that there is a connection between the two, even if he himself—"

"Yes, I saw that. But it might be going a bit too far. There's the Gustav angle. He knows that he's being questioned about the valise, and that he might be implicated in the murder enquiry. There's a tie-up there."

"Never mind that," Irene's father interrupted impatiently. "The question is what you're going to do now. If you don't do something quickly, I tell you straight that I shall. It's as plain as paint that Blinkwell knows what's up, and it looks to me to be one of those times when a gun talks better than the best policeman I ever met."

"You can be sure," the superintendent answered patiently, "we're not going to lose any time; but, if you think a moment, you will see that Kindell has done a great deal to relieve your anxiety— and of course ours—because, after making that offer, Blinkwell will take care that nothing happens to Miss Thurlow which would make it more difficult to carry the bargain through. That is, till he gets our reply. There doesn't seem to me, therefore, to be a special hurry about that. Indeed, unless it should be one which will thoroughly satisfy him, there might be an essential advantage in keeping him in suspense."

He was speaking to Kindell rather than the ambassador as he continued: "We haven't been doing exactly nothing while you've been away. We haven't had any report in yet of the two cars being seen after you left them, though we've got every available man out on that job. But I expect Gustav is being questioned in Paris now, and it's ten to one that he knows something that could put us on the right track. You can bet anything that, if he does, our friends there will find some way of making him talk.

"And we're enquiring about the owners of all the other cars that might have been faked to look like Miss Courtney's. That's an almost certain line of enquiry, though it may not be as quick as the occasion requires.

"Two of the cars of same pattern and colour recently sold were to members of the family of the Earl of Barleigh. There's not much hope there. We already know that one's in a garage in Lancashire. Another's in Belgium. Another belongs to Snacklit, the man who runs the well-known Dogs' Home. There's a chance there, but nobody'd call it good. The Divisional Superintendent says they've never had any complaint against him. Quite the other way. Still, we're taking nothing for granted. We're enquiring about his car now—where it is, and whether it's been out during the day.

"Another car was sold to Sellwell, the stockbroker who failed last August. He's failed twice before, and those little episodes seem to make no difference to his style of living. He's my choice, and an officer will be ringing his bell just about now."

Mr. Thurlow said: "That's what we were arguing when you came in. I say a stockbroker isn't the kind. I don't care whether he's inside the Exchange or out, or whether he fails once a week. The dogs' meat man's my pigeon."

"He isn't a dogs' meat man," the superintendent replied with the calmness that Thurlow had found it so hard to endure; "he keeps a Dogs' Home. Kindness to animals and all that. His father was one of the most famous philanthropists of his time. Still, I've an open mind. It's a startling world. Any minute we may know now."

Even as he spoke, the telephone rang, and his two impatient companions had to wait while he listened silently to a rather long report, at the end of which he only said: "Thanks, Chorley, you've done well. That's about what I expected. You'd better stand by for further orders."

He had scarcely laid down the receiver, and had no time to report what had been said, before the bell rang again, and there was a second report to be received in the same way. And this time his concluding comment, though briefer, was almost in the same words. He only said: "Well, that's that. It's just about what I was expecting to hear."

Then he turned to Thurlow to say, "We've had reports in now about both Snacklit and Sellwell, and if I'd taken the bet you offered, I'm afraid you'd have lost.

"As to Snacklit, he's had his car out during the day. Of course, you'd expect that. It would be more likely than not. But he met our enquiry reasonably, as any decent man would. Gave an account of where he'd been and why, and told us how it could be checked up on if we should wish.

"Our man says he'd had a few words with someone in the yard before he asked to speak to Snacklit himself, and he gave just the same account of where the car had been.

"Sellwell acted differently. I'd put Chorley, one of our best men, on to him. He got into the garage first without being noticed, and he says the engine was still warm, so we know that that car had been out too. And that's all we do know. Chorley said he hadn't spoken a couple of sentences before Sellwell told him to go to hell

"Chorley isn't quick-tempered. He says he tried to take it in a good-humoured way, and get Sellwell to listen, but the man worked himself up into a vile temper, and said that if he didn't get out, he'd get thrown. So he came away, but he had the sense to put a man on to watch the house before reporting to me.

"There's nothing conclusive, of course, in either case; but you can see which of them acted like an innocent man."

"You mean Sellwell, sir?" Kindell asked. He was less sure, but he knew that Allenby was a shrewd officer whose mistakes were few.

"Naturally."

"I wonder—" Kindell began, and stopped.

"Wondering what? You needn't mind saying; even if it were whether I am a fool. You may be sure of that. Superintendents always are."

Allenby smiled as he said this. His reputation was too securely founded for him to be oversensitive to criticism, nor was he of the kind to refuse to listen to a subordinate's views.

"I was just wondering whether you would have judged the two reports quite in the same way if you hadn't had the previous argument."

"That's how it looks to you? Well, whatever I think, we'll follow them both up."

Mr. Thurlow broke in impatiently: "We're getting nowhere. What I want to know is what you're going to do about Blinkwell's offer."

"I couldn't make such a deal on my own authority. Only the Home Secretary could do that. I was on the point of saying that I propose to report the matter to the Assistant Commissioner immediately, and if he thinks that such a bargain should be made he will doubtless lay the whole matter before Mr. Lambton at once. I expect he'll have done that, more or less, already. But, as I said before, I don't think there's any urgency about letting Blinkwell have our reply. While he's waiting, he's sure to be marking time, and that means that he'll be taking particular care of Miss Thurlow while we're pushing our enquiries on."

Mr. Thurlow picked up his hat. "You must go ahead in your own way," he said, "but I'm not hanging about for an hour longer waiting for something to be turned up. I'm going to get Rene home tonight, or someone's going to have a bad time."

"What do you propose to do?"

"See Blinkwell—and a few others, if it's still necessary after that. But I expect to find that he'll be able to do what I want. Kindell, you'll do no good staying here. You'd better come with me, and be a witness of what I do."

Kindell hesitated. He looked at Superintendent Allenby. But that gentleman nodded silent assent. He had no authority to stop Mr. Thurlow, if he were determined to attempt the rescue of his daughter by his own method, and Kindell's company might be advantageous in several ways.

CHAPTER XXXV.

PROFESSOR BLINKWELL IS ROUSED TO WRATH

WHEN PROFESSOR BLINKWELL relayed the message to Snacklit concerning the dog with the bad ear, he was—need it be said?—concerned for himself only. He had already decided that the dog-killer's use was done, and that his liquidation must be quietly arranged so soon as this annoying episode should be ended in a way which past experiences gave him reason for feeling confident that he could contrive.

Neither had he come to a final decision as to what it would be best to do about the girl whom Snacklit had so foolishly guided and admitted to his own premises, after he had allowed her to identify him as the man who had called to collect the case of illicit drugs.

But he saw the necessity of restraining Snacklit from irrevocable action before his own mind should be made up. To defer it might increase Snacklit's risk, if the car should be traced to his door, but Professor Blinkwell was not equally clear that it would increase his own, which was his single concern.

He had a doubtful hope that the police would accept the offer which he had made, in view of the nationality and position of the missing girl, and he saw advantages to himself if he should appear as one who could find and rescue her when they had been foiled. It was not a tale for their own credit that they would wish to have widely known. And there would be her father's gratitude. Something could surely be made of that.

But he saw that it would not be an easy bargain to make or define, and he did not expect to get an immediate reply. Superintendent Allenby's judgment had been sound when he had said that, while the reply was delayed, the Professor would be likely to use his influence in the right way.

That on which Allenby did not calculate, and which was even more surprising to the Professor than it would have been to himself,

160

was that the Professor would find that his authority was not enough. Yet such was the fact.

Snacklit hurried to the telephone in response to the urgent call he received, and was instructed in cryptic words, but such as he could not possibly misunderstand, that Miss Thurlow must be treated with every possible consideration until further orders should be received. Snacklit, worried though he would have been in view of the disappearance of a taxi driver concerning which he would surely have to face a hostile investigation if Irene should be released, would probably have done what he was told, but for what he knew that Irene had seen.

Unfortunately, to narrate this episode was, in spite of its ingenious complexity, beyond the resources of the code he used. He felt that the occurrence itself, joined to his inability to report it, justified some independence of action. Without possibility of such explanation as might, even to Professor Blinkwell's merciless discipline, have gone some way toward condoning his insubordination, he made it clear that he could not undertake to comply with the instructions he had received.

He was curter in this than he might otherwise have been because he was uneasy at having left Irene, which he had not intended to do until he had satisfied himself that she had told him all that she could and he had disposed of her in a final manner, for which his plans had been made.

But Professor Blinkwell received his message with a mingling of astonishment and anger which was not free from an undercurrent of fear. A gang which operates outside the law, which handles large sums of money, and the members of which must depend upon a common loyalty for their own protection, is only held together by ruthless discipline, such as Professor Blinkwell had shown himself able and resolute to enforce. No one knew these facts better than Snacklit, who had been executioner of more than one on whom the Professor had passed sentence of death which might be unknown to the victim until he found himself in the hands of those by whom he would be bound, drugged, and thrust into the asphyxiating chamber, for the existence of which there was such an excellent pretext—or perhaps even thrown into the incinerator without that preliminary, if there should be occasion for haste. Was there not a reason for that incinerator also which all nice-minded people would approve? Who would wish to see a daily heap of dead dogs of all shapes and sizes shovelled into a cart in the open street?

To the Professor's mind the fact that Snacklit should venture upon an insubordinate attitude in the moment of common peril had a note of ominous warning beyond anything he had encountered during this most vexatious episode of his career of well-ordered crime. It brought him to an instant decision to take the matter in hand himself, and carry through the imaginary programme which he had suggested to the consideration of the police. If he should be too late—well, even so, the bold course might be the best. Snacklit might then be silenced—removed—and all trace of what had occurred obliterated, so that the utmost efforts of the police would be exerted vainly to ascertain what had occurred, and with no fear whatever that his own part in it could be more than an ugly doubt.

There might, he admitted to himself in a mind that was not usually hasty in decision, be some possible explanation, some extenuation which Snacklit might be able to urge, in which idea his logical faculty came somewhat near to the fact. But if so, he must know, not guess. The position called imperatively for his control, and it was fortunate that he had already provided himself with an explanation for the police. He was on an errand of rescue on their behalf. That was, if he should be in time, and should decide that Irene should be saved; and, in any case, if they should learn where he was about to go, as they might not do.

With these thoughts in his mind, he rang to order his car, and then got through to Myra's bedroom, to be told in a sleepy voice that his niece had retired for the night.

"Then," he said, "you'd better wake yourself up with a jerk. The quicker you're dressed the better.

"I'm going after that Thurlow girl, and I want you to be up to take any calls that come, particularly if there should be one from me.

"And if Kindell phones or comes back, you're to tell him that I got uneasy as to what might be happening when I heard nothing more from him, and I've gone out again to see whether there's anything more I can do to help."

"He surely wouldn't be coming back at this hour," Myra answered in sulky protest, but she spoke to a dead wire. It would be incredible, even after his experience of the last hour, that there should be rebellion from her.

It was not long after he left the house that she found that she had not reversed the process of her evening toilet in vain.

The American ambassador was announced, and Kindell followed him into the room.

Mr. Thurlow was polite, but abrupt. "It is Professor Blinkwell we wish to see."

"I'm afraid," she answered, "you've come rather too late. But he left a message, in case you should ring up, that he was uneasy about what might be happening, and he has gone out to see what he can do."

"Well, we'd better follow him up. Perhaps you can tell us where we should be most likely to find him."

"I'm sorry: he didn't say."

"But you could make a good guess?" the ambassador persisted.

Kindell, who knew Myra's tone of sincerity, thought that she was speaking the truth for once, and that it would be useless to press her further. He was not surprised when she repeated: "I'm sorry: I've no idea. He didn't say a word about it."

But Mr. Thurlow had not finished. He asked, with the abruptness he had first used, "It wouldn't by any chance be a Dogs' Home?"

Myra was a practised and skilful liar, and she had, in fact, no particular reason for supposing that her uncle had gone to Snacklit's, being ignorant of the concluding events of the day. But the question startled her by its suggestion of a knowledge she had not supposed that they would have had.

In half a second she had voice and expression under control, and said, with some trace of natural annoyance: "I keep telling you that I've no idea where. He's sure to be back before long. Would you like to wait?"

But in that half-second Kindell had seen the startled fear in her eyes. He heard the ambassador say curtly: "No, we won't wait. We'll be getting on." As they left the house together, he said, "I suppose it's the Dogs' Home now?"

"Yes," the ambassador replied grimly. "I reckon I should have won that bet. But I wonder what they've done with Rene there?"

"Know the Snacklit Dogs' Home?" he asked the taxi driver "Then here's a pound note, and don't stop for the lights if there's a way through."

"Right you are, guv'nor," the man said cheerfully, and headed his car to the destination to which one of his fraternity had already gone that day on a journey from which there was no return.

CHAPTER XXXVI.

THE POKER, OR ELSE THE BELL

SNACKLIT LOOKED AT the three whose conversation his entrance had abruptly stopped, and there was suspicion in his eyes. Neither Kate nor Billson were, he had good reason to believe, aware of his more sinister activities. Kate was a household servant, engaged through a Labour Exchange a few months before, at a wage sufficiently high to make it a place she would be reluctant to leave.

Billson was employed in the business. He acted as porter, he worked the lift, he was the routine executioner of the dogs and cats, and any other domestic creatures who had tired the patience of their owners by illness or age, or making it difficult to close their owners' houses.

Snacklit had told him that a young woman had called of whose honesty he was not sure, and that he was not to allow her to leave the premises unless she should be shown out in a regular manner. That had been both a precaution against Irene getting away through the front entrance and a means of keeping Billson in that part of the premises while other things were happening elsewhere of which it was desirable that he should not know.

Had Snacklit foreseen that he would have that telephone call which he could not ignore, he would have made different arrangements. Now he looked round in a well-founded doubt of what might have been said while he was away.

His anxiety and the sense of urgency under which he acted were increased by the fact that he did not return only from receiving and refusing Professor Blinkwell's telephone instructions. He had also interviewed the detective sergeant whom Superintendent Allenby had sent to the house. He thought he had been successful in turning that enquiry aside; but it had been a plain warning of the activity of the police—of an enquiry which might be concentrating upon him. Suppose they had come with a search warrant, and had discovered her there—had listened to what she certainly would have said—had looked into the furnace while the taxi driver's bones were still recognizable? There was no time for further hesitation now. He asked, "What's been happening here?"

Kate would have answered, but Billson was quicker than she. He said: "Kate just called me in, sir. I don't know why."

Kate explained: "The young lady said she wanted to go, so I called Billson. You told me to, if she did."

Irene saw that, though they might not be prepared to give her further support, they did not betray what she had said, and she got some small comfort from that.

Snacklit said, "Well, you can both go now."

Irene became aware that she was desperately afraid of what might happen if she should be left alone with Snacklit again. She said, "They're not going without me."

"I suppose," Snacklit retorted, "I can give orders in my own house."

"You can't give orders to me. I say, if they go out of the room, I go too. If I'm kept here, I mean to be able to tell the police who's in it and who's not."

The two servants had stood hesitating, evidently interested in what they heard. Snacklit looked at them angrily. Billson said, "Come alone, Kate." He put his hand on her arm and drew her out of the room.

Irene would have followed, but Snacklit was too quick for her. He was first at the door, turned the key, and dropped it into his pocket. He faced her, scowling. Here was a fresh reason for doubt. If she were traced to the house (but was that likely?), how much would those two say, if they should be questioned? How safely could they be bribed? Neither of them was of high character. But their degree of loyalty to him might not be great. It was an added risk, but still, if she could be done away with completely without their knowledge, was it not still the one path on which a prospect of safety lay?

"Now," he said, "if you value your skin, you'll sit down quietly and tell me what you really know, or think you know, and what made you follow me in the way you did."

"And if you value your skin, you'll unlock the door. I shan't tell you anything till the key's back where it belongs,"

"You'll wait a long time, if you wait for that," he said "but I've no time to lose. If you won't talk sensibly to me, I shall have to send for someone who'll treat you differently than I was meaning to do."

As he said this, his eyes were on the bell. Irene, having declined his suggestion that she should sit down, was standing near the fireplace. He would have to come close to her to reach the bell push.

Her own eyes had settled for a moment upon a heavy metal ornament on the mantelpiece. She judged its weight, and the distance between them. She had attended a college where baseball was not unknown. She thought she could manage that.

"I'll give you one last chance," she said. "If you don't open the door—"

He laughed, and advanced towards her, with a purpose she did not understand, but to which she saw only one sufficient reply. She seized the heavy ornament, and threw with all the force of her desperation and of a young and vigorous arm. Snacklit ducked, or he would have been worse hurt than he was. But the attack had been so sudden and unexpected that he was not quick enough to avoid it entirely.

It did not come full in his face, as had been intended, but it struck him a glancing blow, and he fell forward.

She knew the pocket in which he had put the key. She had it out as he tried dizzily to rise. Seeing what she had done, he snatched at her catching an arm. He was still half-dazed by the blow, but he tried to drag her toward the grate. She misunderstood his intention, and, instead of trying to keep him away, she struggled to be first there. She succeeded in her own aim, which she had supposed to have been his. She caught the poker in her free hand, but as she did so he rose sufficiently to press the lower of the two bell pushes beside the grate.

The next moment the poker came down hard on the hand that held her, and she was free.

She had dropped the key in the struggle, and must come near him to look for it in the thick rug. He was still only raised on one hand, but he made a sudden grab at her foot, pulling her down.

At that, in a passion of mingled anger and fear, she struck hard and blindly with the poker across his face. He screamed at the blow, and fell back. "Burfoot!" he called. "Burfoot!" and then tried again to rise and pursue her, as he saw that she was taking no further notice of him, but had already got the key into the door.

"You hell cat!" he said. "You don't know how you're going to pay for this." He stood swaying, wiping the blood from his face. He thought his cheekbone was broken. He spat out blood and a broken tooth.

Irene stood at the open door, where Burfoot blocked her way. She knew him both as the man who had driven the grey car and, more certainly, as one of those who had wheeled the hand-cart across the garden.

Even with the short poker in her hand, she did not feel that she would be equal to a struggle with him, nor was she used to settling her differences in such a manner.

She took a step back, letting him enter the room. Conventional standards of conduct became dominant again as she said in explanation, and in a voice that was almost apologetic: "I couldn't help it. He wouldn't let me get out of the room."

The man looked stolidly at his injured master, and then at her. She was uncertain how he would take it, until he said brutally: "You'll get your neck wrung if you try any games with me." His eyes were evil, but his lips grinned, as though the idea of her resisting him were an enjoyable joke.

Snacklit said: "You'll know what's got to be done with her after this. You can call Wilkes, if you need help. Better keep the others out of it, if you can."

Irene said boldly: "You won't call anyone, if you're a wise man. I'm going to give a hundred pounds to whoever gets me out of here, and you may as well have the lot." She added, seeing no sign of change in his expression, "The police may be here any minute, and you'd rather I say you're one of those who were helping me to get out."

"Tom, she's lying," Snacklit interposed. "But if it's true, you can't be too quick. She saw you and Wilkes crossing the lawn."

The man appeared to take no notice. He said slowly: "You'd give me a hundred pounds? You'd do that if I let you go quiet by the side door?"

"You can come with me, if you like, and you shall have it as soon as I get home."

Snacklit said angrily: "Don't take any notice of what she says. She'll be your death, if you do."

Burfoot made no answer to that. He turned back to the door. "If you'll come with me, miss," he said, in a more civil voice than he had used before, "I'll show you the way out. But I'd put that poker back. You won't want to carry it through the streets."

He had winked at his master as he turned round, and Snacklit said no more. He gave his attention again to his bleeding face, which was now darkened by a long bruise, lividly blue.

But an ugly smile came painfully to his face as Irene followed the man through the door. He thought that full payment would soon be made.

CHAPTER XXXVII.

THE HOME SECRETARY WANTS TO KNOW

THE HOME SECRETARY had to wait. He was told that Superintendent Allenby was on the Paris telephone, and could not be interrupted, even for him. Impatient though he might be, he had to wait for some time. When he got connected at last, he said: "I want to know just what the position is, and what's being done. I can't think how you could allow matters to get into such a position."

"You mean about Miss Thurlow?"

"Yes, and His Excellency. Where are they now? I hope you're not going to tell me that you don't know."

"We don't know for certain where Miss Thurlow is yet. Her father's out looking for her, with a gun in his hip pocket."

"You mean you've—?"

"We've done all we could, of course. And there's still some reason to think it may turn out all right.

"But there's fresh information just come in from Paris, and the question is really for you, sir. What you think it will be best for us to do. They've got a waiter detained there who's made a statement that Professor Blinkwell murdered Reynard, because he was on the point of revealing to Mr. Thurlow that Blinkwell had got some device for smuggling drugs through with the ambassador's luggage without his knowledge."

"You mean Blinkwell, the director of Vantons? It sounds incredible."

"I should say it's true, more likely than not. Blinkwell was certainly at the hotel. And someone finally did get the drugs through in that way, though it was by a different trick from the one that Gustav—that's the waiter—says they were first going to use.

"But to say it's probably true isn't to say it can be proved. There's only Gustav's word, and he gave another version before, which we know was all lies.

"Anyway, the Sûreté seem to have their tails in the air. They say they're sending through the extradition papers at once, and they want us to fetch Blinkwell in before he can get word of what's going on."

"Well, they've a right to ask that. Whether they'll get the extradition depends, of course, on what evidence they can produce. And that's a matter for the court to decide. I'm not concerned about that. It's the American—"

"But that's just where the difficulty comes in. Blinkwell's made an offer, almost in plain words, to hand over Miss Thurlow if we promise to leave him and his gang alone. Of course, he doesn't call it his gang, but I should say that's what it is. The question is, if we arrest him now, how's it going to affect that?"

"You know where Blinkwell is now?"

"Not exactly. We know that Thurlow went to his house and was out again in about three minutes, driving almost certainly to a Dogs' Home in Hampstead. I should say there'll be quite a party there before long."

"You mean you let His Excellency—"

"I couldn't have stopped him without knocking him down. We've got a good man—not one of the regular force—in his car with him. And there's another car following him wherever he goes, though he isn't likely to know that. Besides that, when I heard which way he was heading, I sent a squad straight to Snacklit's place. That's the Dogs' Home. I saw them off just before I took the Paris call. They ought to be there by now."

"Well, I expect you've done all you could. We must just hope for the best. I suppose we shall soon know."

"Yes, sir, I think we have. And as to pulling Blinkwell in—"

"I shouldn't do that, unless you think it will help you in this matter. I want you to put the Thurlows' interests first. Get them out of it, and then—"

"Yes, sir, I understand."

Mr. Lambton said that he had no doubt of that. He wished to be rung up instantly if anything of importance should occur. Not to his secretary. Not through the Commissioner. Allenby was to report to him direct. He would be at the House for the next two hours, if not three.

CHAPTER XXXVIII.

THE INCIDENTS OF AN ACTIVE HOUR

IF WE SHOULD be disposed to consider that some of those concerned acted with extreme folly and disregard for almost certain consequences to themselves during the hour with which we are now dealing, we should give due weight to the fact that no one but the three concerned were aware of the conversation which had occurred between Irene, Kate, and Billson. And if we should go on to analyse cause and effect, and to observe the perverse results of the most cautious and intelligent courses, we may see the origin of all that followed in the telephone message from Professor Blinkwell, which caused Snacklit to leave Irene, to which the action of Allenby in sending an officer to enquire concerning Snacklit's car must be added, as it prolonged Snacklit's absence from the room.

The long façade of Snacklit House had three entrances. One was closed by the wide gates into the yard. One, the central and most imposing, was that which gave access to the business premises, where dogs and other animals could be bought, or deposited for hospital treatment, or for the destruction of which it was etiquette to speak so delicately, and which was so discreetly, expeditiously, and thoroughly done.

Beyond that was the entrance to the philanthropist's private residence. It had an appearance of modesty, disguising the fact that it led to luxurious apartments which crossed the complete length of the rear of the building, both at its first and second floors.

Professor Blinkwell, who knew the place, directed his chauffeur to drive to the private entrance, and to wait for him there. He did not intend there should be any appearance of his having made a furtive visit. He acted on his usual principle of conforming to the natural conduct of a man whose conscience is well at ease. In the past, he had found it to be a method which served him well.

170

Kate was the one who normally opened the door, as she did now. Billson was in charge of the main entrance, which was closed at this hour, but there was another reason why he was not on the scene, to which we shall come.

Kate took the Professor's name, which was strange to her. She knew that customers came at all hours, and such she took him to be. She asked him to take a seat in the hall, and went to give Snacklit his name. The Professor gave her a ten yards' start, and then followed her. The carpets were soft and thick and she did not hear him until she had knocked at the door of her master's room. He was close behind her then. He said: "All right, my good girl. I can manage now." She thought it discreet to withdraw.

Snacklit called, "Come in," in a voice of irritation, and stared in surprise unmixed with pleasure when he saw who it was who entered. The Professor looked equally surprised at the condition of the man upon whom he intruded with so little ceremony.

Snacklit lay back on a settee. There was a swelling on the side of his head where it had been first hit, and the black bruise, streaked with drying blood, had now spread over half his face. He held a reddened towel, with which he was still wiping blood from his mouth.

"You seem," the Professor said coldly, "to have been making a mess of things, or perhaps I should say that they have been making a mess of you."

"It's that she-devil who's been handling the stuff," Snacklit answered. "She looked as though a mouse could have made her jump, but you never know."

"Well," the Professor answered, "you shouldn't have brought her here. It was the act of a fool, and I've come to see what can be done now."

"I didn't bring her. She followed me."

"We won't argue that. The question is: where she is now?"

"She's where she'll be no more trouble to us. Burfoot's seeing to that."

"You mean—"

"Yes. She went off with him like a lamb." Snacklit's face was contorted into a difficult smile at the recollection.

"How long ago was this?"

"Ten minutes. Maybe a bit more."

"Then it would be too late to interfere?"

"That's a safe guess."

"Then we won't attempt it. After all, it may be the best way. But I had told you—"

"You didn't know that she'd seen the taxi man after he'd been knocked on the head?"

"Did she? That was certainly an argument for ruling a double line. But it is a matter on which I must be sure that there has been no further mistake. I should like to see her before I go."

"She'd be a queer sight by now."

"It will be one that I can endure. She would still, I suppose, be in the gas chamber?"

"I don't know that. Burfoot wouldn't lose any time. He might have her in the furnace by now."

"So I expect he will. I have been informed that he is both thorough and energetic in all he does. Perhaps you will show me the way there? I should like to see for myself, and after that the incident shall not be mentioned between us again."

On this assurance, which sounded satisfactory to him, and in saying which the Professor had spoken with a literal sincerity which he did not always employ, Snacklit rose and led the way down the corridor, and by a back stair to the walled enclosure beside the garden in which the incinerator was built.

"You have," Professor Blinkwell remarked, as they approached it, "a furnace of ample size."

Mr. Snacklit was gratified by this recognition, so that he almost forgot the pains he was enduring as he replied that it was his policy to be ready for all emergencies. There were occasions when a large number of dogs had to be destroyed in a short time. It would be objectionable to keep them lying about, as might happen in smaller and less efficient establishments. And the proportion of large dogs (such as Great Danes and mastiffs) which were offered for his ministrations (probably owing to the cost of their food) was high.

As he completed this explanation, they reached the door of the furnace, where the man Wilkes, of whom we have seen nothing except that brief moment when he shared the labour of wheeling the dead taxi driver across the garden, and of whom we know nothing beyond the negative fact that he had not got red hair, was standing by.

Snacklit asked, "Anything special put into the furnace just lately?"

Wilkes may not have known what answer he was expected to give. Anyway, he was discreet in his reply, "I haven't noticed that close."

Snacklit didn't press the point. He said, "I think Professor Blinkwell would like to look in."

Wilkes picked up a long-handled hook and drew back the sliding door. The furnace roared in their faces.

Whether Professor Blinkwell wanted to look or not, Snacklit certainly did. He went forward, blinking into the white heat.

"I can't see anything of her," he said. "Or at least, not to be sure. Nothing could last long in that heat."

Professor Blinkwell said: "No, I suppose not." What he gave Snacklit could not fairly be called a kick. It was a mere push with his foot, well judged and well placed. With a shrill scream the man fell forward into the fire.

"You'd better close the shutter," the Professor said. "He's not pleasant to watch."

Wilkes said no more than, "You're the boss." The hook came into operation again.

CHAPTER XXXIX.

AN OBJECTION TO BEING ROASTED ALIVE

"I DON'T THINK this is the way out." There was panic in Irene's voice which she could not control.

Burfoot had stopped and locked the door through which they had come. There might be no certain significance in that, but he was now leading the way to a glass-walled chamber, the use of which was not difficult to guess, even apart from the faint penetrating odour which never left its precincts, even when it was not charged with the fumes by which it destroyed its countless unsuspecting victims, who were repaid for the love and loyalty they had given to men by this murderous treachery.

Burfoot looked at her with the derisive grin she had seen at their first encounter. He said: "You can please yourself. It's all one to me. But I should say a good whiff of gas is better than being roasted alive."

"But—you can't mean it!" she answered faintly. "You said you'd show me the way out, and I'd give you a hundred pounds. Suppose we say two? Or what do you want? It's no use trying to frighten me like this. You can't want to be hanged. I've told you the police are on the way here. I know they are."

She stopped before the malicious amusement in his eyes. Incredible as it must seem, she knew at that moment that he meant to kill her, and that there was no hope in any pleading, and little in appeals, either to greed or fear.

The inclination to faint came again, as it had done in the room above, and she knew that, if she should do so, there would be no return to consciousness, unless it should be in some horror of mortal pain.

She looked at the man, who was a head taller than herself massive, muscular, able to break her back over his knee, and she knew that, even if she had retained the poker that she had been cajoled into laying down so foolishly, it would have been useless to her. Her wits must save her, or nothing would. And how could her wits avail?

The man had listened to her with no sign of relenting. She saw that her terror was amusement to him—that he would find pleasure in that which he was meaning to do. But he answered her, in the tone of one who would show sense to a fool: "You didn't think we should let you live? You know a damned sight too much for that."

"If I knew that you had saved my life, wouldn't that be a good thing for you?"

It was shrewdly suggested. For one moment he may have hesitated as to whether it would not be best to take whatever money she might promise now and afterwards prove able and willing to pay, and to take the credit of saving her from Snacklit's hands. But would it save him? It is no sufficient legal defence to say that you declined to kill a young lady at night, if it can be proved against you that you helped to murder a taxi driver at any earlier hour. No, there was one way, and only one, that was sure. And then there was the noise of a key turning in a locked door, and Billson stood in the entrance.

For a moment the three stood looking at one another in silence. Then Billson said: "Kate thought this was about how it'd be. But I'm not standing for it. It's a bit too thick. You should have left the key in the lock if you didn't want me to come butting in."

Burfoot cursed to himself. It was true that he had not given a thought to the duplicate keys that always hung in the outer hall— those that Billson, who did the routine killing, was accustomed to use. And he was not a quick-witted man. He was used to carrying out the orders of others, not to plan for himself.

"It's the master's orders," he said at last. "You'd better talk it over with him."

"Yes. I'll do that. He'll have to know that we don't stand for murder, not Kate or I. You'd better come and hear what I've got to say."

"We'll wait here till you get back."

"Mr. Billson," Irene exclaimed, in a fresh access of terror, "you're not going to leave me here?"

"No, I won't do that. And I've changed my mind about seeing the master. We'll clear out without any more words."

He had guessed that, if he should leave them together, there would be no change in the programme that he had interrupted—and, after that, was it likely that he would be allowed to escape? He remembered Wilkes, a man as powerful and perhaps even more brutal than the one who confronted him now. If he should go upstairs, he might come down to find that Kate had been already dealt with, and that he had to face two men as desperate, and each as strong as himself.

One, at least, had become desperate now. Burfoot said, "No, you don't." His arm swept round, striking Irene with a force which threw her against the wall, from which she collapsed on to the floor. He leapt forward. "You yellow rat!" he cried savagely, as his left shot outward for Billson's chin.

It was a blow which might have been decisive, but Billson swerved, and it did no more than graze the side of his head. It was returned next moment with equal force and more smashing contact, and then the two men fought like raging beasts, while Irene struggled to her feet, to be swept off them again by a rush which was regardless of her.

She tried to dodge the quick movements of the combatants to get past them and through the door, but it was not easy to do without taking the risk of blows which were not intended for her and which she would have been less fit to endure than were those upon whom they fell.

But as she watched for the moment of clear passage that she required, there came what may have been the most welcome sound that her ears had heard—her father's voice calling her name, as he hurried along the passage at a pace which left Kate behind, whose part it had been to show him the way.

"Hands up!" he cried sharply, pulling out the weapon on which he had learnt to rely during the adventurous passage of earlier years. But he spoke to those who were too fully engaged upon their own affairs to heed a summons that was less familiar to their ears than it had been to those of his native state.

Even to one of his emphatic habits, exasperated as he was by the sight of a dishevelled daughter at the further side of the room, it was not a possible programme to make indiscriminate slaughter of the struggling men, one of whom must presumably be his daughter's champion, though he had no clue to which it might be. So they survived the peril natural to those who ignore the customary American greeting.

But though he did not immediately empty the contents of his gun into their contending bodies, he was in no mood to wait patiently for the struggle, which had become an all-out wrestling match rather than a fight, to proceed to its natural end.

Watching his chance, he interposed an adroit foot, which brought Billson heavily to the ground. His opponent found himself confronted by a new antagonist, and a levelled gun. The sharp order, "Stand back, or you're a dead man," came in a tone which the wildest person would be unlikely to disregard. Burfoot did not raise his hands, but they dropped to his sides. Scowling and breathing hard, he backed toward the sliding glass partition of the lethal chamber.

He made no resistance when Kindell, who had entered immediately behind the ambassador, passed a precautionary hand over his pockets.

"Irene, are you all right?" her father asked, without taking his eyes off the two men, the second of whom had now risen from the floor, and was using the back of his hand to improve the sight of a blackened and bleeding eye. "Then you'd better tell me who's who in this mix-up."

"It's the one you've got covered," Irene replied with ungrammatical lucidity. "He was trying to kill me. Mr. Billson was trying to get me away. I think we owe him a hundred pounds."

It was an opportune testimonial, for the police, whose coming Irene had foretold on such dubious grounds, were now crowding into the room.

"Do you charge this man?" a detective sergeant asked briskly.

"I charge him with trying to murder me," Irene said, with a fierce hatred in her heart which is easy to understand, "and with helping to kill the driver who brought me here."

"That's enough to go on with," the sergeant answered.

"It was just a bit of a game," the man said sullenly. "And what about what she'd done before? Bashed Mr. Snacklit's head with a poker before I got her away."

But as he spoke the handcuffs were on his wrists, and Mr. Thurlow was putting away a gun which had done its part. As he did so, the voice of Professor Blinkwell gave some confirmation to the allegation that Burfoot had made. "It is certainly true that Mr. Snacklit has been rather badly hurt, but, from admissions which he made to me a few moments ago, I should say he brought it upon himself, and Miss Thurlow did no more than was justified by the detention to which she was subjected."

The reception of this statement, and the general consciousness of his entrance which it brought, was certainly without warmth, but the Professor showed no consciousness of that. The sergeant said only, "I'd better see Mr. Snacklit. Where is he now?"

"I left him," Professor Blinkwell answered, "in the lounge upstairs. He was resting on a couch there, his face being badly injured. From what he told me, I felt that Miss Thurlow might be requiring assistance. I found this man"—he looked at Wilkes standing somewhat in the rear, as he said this—"in the back premises, and he guided me here."

With the same absence of comment, the sergeant said, "You'd better show me where Snacklit is."

The Professor showed no unwillingness to oblige, but when they reached the lounge, it will be readily believed that Mr. Snacklit was not there.

CHAPTER XL.

PROFESSOR BLINKWELL WAS PLEASED

MR. LAMBTON RECEIVED Superintendent Allenby's report before leaving the House, and it went far to relieve his mind. The American Ambassador had returned to Grosvenor Square with a daughter who had been no more than superficially damaged, and without having involved himself in any further homicidal episodes. International amity seemed unlikely to be disturbed.

So far, so good; but there were other aspects of the matter such as might still lead the most cautious Secretary to make one of those blunders which cause the Home Office to be regarded as the most perilous stage of a climbing politician's career.

Allenby ended his report by saying: "Snacklit made himself scarce, knocked about though he certainly was, as soon as our men entered the building. It's difficult to guess how it was done, as we had every exit watched. It looks as though he'd got a getaway planned beforehand, and when he knew we were there, he saw that the game was up. Anyway, it was pleading guilty in a loud voice, and he shouldn't take long to catch. Not with his face marked as it is."

Mr. Lambton said he supposed not. What arrests had actually been made?

"Only the man Burfoot. It'll be a long stretch, if not the gallows, for him. We've brought another man named Wilkes in for questioning, but we haven't gone further than that. There are one or two others who won't leave Snacklit House without our having something to say. But I told Sergeant Duckworth to go slow till we'd thought it out."

"Quite right. What about Blinkwell?"

"We've done nothing so far. We've not got much to go on. And I didn't know what you would wish. Of course, there are those extradition papers on the way. We can't ignore them."

"No, they can't be ignored, but there's no need to do more to-night. I'll see Sir Henry in the morning and talk it over with him."

Mr. Lambton, his mind greatly relieved, though not unaware of further problems ahead, went home for a short night's sleep.

But Allenby had still instructions to give, such as would keep some of his best men busy through the night, and then, before leaving for his own neglected bed, he gave orders that Professor Blinkwell should be rung up at an early hour, with a request to call during the morning at Scotland Yard, "Not before ten-thirty, or say ten-forty-five, We ought to know where we are by then." By that time he would have Sir Henry's instructions. He would have spoken to the Sûreté again. It was possible that the extradition papers would be on his desk.

Professor Blinkwell was punctual. It was exactly ten-forty-four when he stepped out of his car, and he was shown up to Superintendent Allenby's room without delay.

"It was good of you," he said as he entered, "to ring me up. But I should, in any case, have given you a call this morning. It appeared to me that you ought to know just what I saw and heard at Snacklit's House, though I am not sure that it will be of material assistance to your investigations. But that is for you to decide."

"Yes."

"You will like to have what I say taken down?"

"Sergeant Temple is doing that."

Professor Blinkwell looked at the officer seated at the further end of the room as though he had not observed him before. "It is a good method," he said. "It saves both repetitions and doubt."

"Yes. You know Snacklit?"

"It is a matter of how you use the word. He consulted me some time ago regarding the composition of a gas which he is accustomed to use. At that time he struck me as a humane man."

"When was that?"

"The date may be of importance? It is hard to see how. But in that case I should prefer to consult my diary before I reply."

"Approximately?"

"If you please, I prefer accuracy. I will consult my diary and let you know."

"You might help us materially if you would say what drew your suspicions in his direction?"

For the first time, the Professor showed signs of embarrassment. "I was afraid," he said, "that you would ask that. It was through a private matter, which I should prefer not to explain."

"I am afraid I must press it."

He still hesitated. "Kindell," he said at last, "is an attractive young man."

"Yes. What of that?"

"And I have a niece who is still young. Miss Thurlow is younger."

"No doubt she is. But I fail to see—"

"Mr. Kindell had engagements he did not, and perhaps could not, explain. You understand that better than I. Curiosity was aroused."

"You are explaining nothing at all."

"Perhaps jealousy would be a more adequate word."

"Perhaps it might. But I still fail to see—"

"Is it necessary that you should? What I desired to convey was that curiosity—or jealousy—being aroused, things were noticed—perhaps I should say discovered, which would otherwise—I think I must have made myself sufficiently clear."

"No, I can't say that you have. What I asked was what had first caused you to suspect Snacklit."

"I am afraid that I must decline to be more specific. I may already have said too much. And it is not, in fact, an explanation that could help you at all. What I thought I ought to tell you is what occurred when I reached Snacklit House, a short while before Mr. Thurlow intervened, perhaps more effectually than I should have been able to do."

"You don't mind our questioning Miss Blinkwell?"

"About what I have said? It would be a gaucherie which I should regret, but it would not be within my power to prevent. If you would imply that it might disclose some indiscretion of mine—which is absurd—no, I should not object at all."

"Very well. Then we will come to what happened at Snacklit House."

"I saw Mr. Snacklit in the lounge on the first floor. The girl whom I afterwards heard called Kate showed me up, or, at least would have announced me, but I followed her without waiting for that.

"I found him on the couch, his face very badly cut and discoloured, and my first question was naturally to enquire how he had come to be in such a condition. He said something about a hellcat, or some such word, and I replied that Miss Thurlow would certainly not have committed such an act unless the provocation had been extreme. It was a shot in the dark, but it went home.

"He looked frightened, and, I thought, conscious for the first time of the indiscretion of what he had said before. He said something about not knowing what I meant, and I became seriously alarmed as I considered the kind of scene which must have occurred, and how he could have disposed of her subsequently.

"I told him that I was enquiring for Miss Thurlow, and that, in view of his condition, and what he had said about it already, it was useless to profess ignorance.

"I said that I had no wish to create any disturbance and, in view of the punishment he had received, nothing more might be said about the matter, if he would allow me to take her quietly away.

"He said I could take anyone away as far as he was concerned, but as he didn't know who I was talking about, he couldn't say more than that.

"I told him that I must take that as permission to search the house, and he told me to go to hell.

"He gave me the impression of a man who was in such a state of combined mental desperation and physical pain that he was hardly conscious of what he said.

"I left him then and went down some back stairs, and found myself in a lighted passage. I went along that, and came to a large incinerator built out from the house, and a man was there stoking up."

"You mean Wilkes?"

"I did not have occasion to ask his name."

"We arrested him for murder an hour ago."

"From his appearance and manner I cannot say that it is an incredible charge. But when I told him that I was looking for a young lady who was known to be on the premises, he said he could probably take me to the right place, and that he certainly did.

"I must find some satisfaction in thinking that I should almost certainly have been in time, even if Mr. Thurlow had not been there, though I might not have been able to intervene so effectually, and what assistance I might have received from Wilkes can be a matter of conjecture only."

"You say you left Snacklit on the couch in the lounge?"

"Yes."

"He showed no sign of following you?"

"No. Nor did he look equal to doing it. I should have said that he was incapable of great exertion. He might, of course, have got into a car."

"We know he didn't do that."

"Am I to conclude that it was for his murder that you have arrested Wilkes?"

"Not at all. We have no reason to suppose that he has been murdered, but the man who drove Miss Thurlow certainly was. She saw his body being wheeled to the incinerator, and when we drew the fire there were obvious human remains, which a few further hours would have reduced to unrecognizable ashes. No doubt it was done on Snacklit's orders, and that's probably why he disappeared in the way he did."

"Do I understand," the Professor asked, "that the heat of the incinerator would be sufficient to destroy a human body—even the bones—beyond recognition within so short a time?"

"Yes, that is so. The wonder really was that we were able to secure such definite evidence after the time which had elapsed. But you can understand why Wilkes was busy stoking the fire."

Professor Blinkwell said that that was certainly what he would be likely to do. He observed silently (it was not a matter to be spoken aloud) that Wilkes and Burfoot would probably be most justly hanged—as in fact they were—for the murder of the taxi driver, on the unjust evidence of the remains of Mr. Snacklit which the furnace had been allowed insufficient time to consume entirely. Would Wilkes try to save himself by asserting the truth that it was Snacklit's body, and that Professor Blinkwell had pushed him in? It would be a most improbable thing, and, even if it were believed, it would be worse than useless to him, for he would have to admit that he had done nothing to intervene or denounce the crime. It would be to make his fate sure, even beyond the faint hope of reprieve which may follow conviction for the foulest crime, if a doubt of guilt, however slender, can be suggested to the Home Secretary's mind.

Mr. Allenby rose. With a toneless formality, he thanked Professor Blinkwell for the information he had given. Actually he saw no reason to doubt its substantial accuracy, apart only from the nature and extent of his knowledge of Snacklit, and his reasons for supposing that Irene would have been in his hands.

Professor Blinkwell rose also. He spoke with simple sincerity when he said that there was no occasion for thanks. Whatever little he had been able to do at Snacklit House had been a pleasure to him.

CHAPTER XLI.

BUT MYRA FELT DIFFERENTLY

IT WAS TEN days later that the ambassador gave a dinner to some prominent Englishman whom his country desired to honour.

It was the first day after her experiences at Snacklit House on which Irene had been visible at the Embassy; some physical blemishes, which had been reductive of her usual charms, had prompted an anonymous visit to a South Coast town, which it is better to leave unmentioned, owing to an experience she had there—one of the dubious consequences of anonymity—of which she thought it best that her father should not be told.

Her health, owing to the buoyant quality of her sanguine youth, had been unaffected throughout, and, when this evening came, she showed no trace of the experiences she had undergone excepting an inconspicuous scar near her left eye; and that she would have had the patience to remain secluded until that should disappear would have been an extreme improbability, even apart from the event which we must not be drawn aside to observe, beyond the discreet allusion already made.

To the only guest who was audibly curious concerning the cause of the injury, she replied, with impregnable veracity, that it is always foolish to collide with open doors in the dark, and having put that enquiry so lightly aside, she proceeded to enjoy herself as much as is possible to an ambassador's daughter who shares the responsibility of entertaining her father's guests.

Her right-hand neighbour at the dinner table was a professor of economics of international reputation, and she concluded soundly that he would not be overwhelmingly interested in the knitting of jumpers or the style of the season's hats.

On the other hand, her knowledge of economics was not sufficient to give reasonable hope that she could sustain a conversation upon them without exposing greater ignorance than a hostess prefers to show, and with this consciousness, and that of her international duty of entertaining her guest with a suitable topic of conversation, her mind naturally turned to a subject which had largely occupied it during the voluntary seclusion of the previous week. She introduced the question of the desirability of the marriage of cousins with the verbal adroitness which few men and most women have.

Its connection with economics (if any) is remote, but the old gentleman was one of those numerous specialists who, having succeeded in establishing a reputation for good crowing on their own dunghills, consider that any other should do equally well; and he was, more exceptionally, of wide interests and an unprejudiced mind.

He rose to the bait at once. He said that, like many popular beliefs, the objection to such marriages was only conditionally true. Like to unlike is the law of physical attraction, and cousins are likely but not certain to combine like qualities, both good and bad. The question, should cousins marry, is therefore incapable of absolute reply. Some should, and others should not. A minority of cousins are widely different in temperaments and physique, and, in such cases, if they should both be in good health, their unions might be particularly successful. Nothing can alter the arithmetical fact that the children of first cousins will have less than the normal number of grandparents, and the one who is duplicated may have an abnormally strong influence either, or perhaps both, for good and evil.

The learned doctor having a rather penetrating voice, which was more frequently exercised in the classroom than at the fireside, and the guests not being numerous, his remarks gained the attention of a silent table.

A discussion followed, exposing some differences of opinion, but nothing was said to disturb Irene's opinion that the learned doctor was a most able man.

Mr. Thurlow, listening without comment at the other end of the table, concluded that if Will Kindell were asked to dinner his daughter would not be vexed, and being a man of prompt action when his decisions were clearly made, he telephoned him next morning, and found, without surprise, that his invitation was promptly accepted.

Kindell came that evening, and found that the ambassador and his daughter were dining alone.

Mr. Thurlow explained that he had asked him because he was curious to know what was being done by the police to secure the conviction of Professor Blinkwell (to whom he alluded in language unfitting for the lips of an Envoy Extraordinary and Minister Plenipotentiary of the august country he represented) for his countless crimes, and he enquired with a more personal anxiety to what extent Irene was likely to be involved in the criminal proceedings which had become obviously unavoidable.

"We don't want," he said, "more publicity than we can't help, but we know the mistakes we've made, and I want Allenby to understand that there'll be no squealing from me."

"I told the superintendent that I should see you tonight," Kindell replied, "and he authorized me to say that, so far as Irene is concerned, unless you should wish to prosecute, in which case every facility will, of course, be given, it is not proposed that any action be taken.

"The men principally concerned—Snacklit and Burfoot—are accused, with Wilkes, of the more serious crime of the murder of the taxi driver, and Snacklit has disappeared."

"They expect to apprehend him?"

"With his face in the state it is, I should say, if he has forty-eight-hours' run, he'll be an exceptionally lucky man. But if he doesn't get caught by this time tomorrow, it's an open secret that there'll be a sufficient reward offered to make it sure that someone will give him away.

"It isn't only the murder. There's no doubt that he's been up to his neck in the drug racket, and the chance of ending that is too good to miss.

"That's the common-sense view of the matter, though there's one man on it—Inspector Dunchurch—who's been arguing that we shan't find him, because it was his body of which the remains were in the furnace."

"That sound improbable. But he has some theory to support it?"

"He has the fact that when the ashes were sifted some buttons were found which bear the name of Snacklit's tailor. There'd be more in that if it hadn't been the usual procedure to give Wilkes rubbish and refuse of every kind to burn in the furnace. The most natural explanation is that some old garment had been thrown in, perhaps after it had been used as a rag."

"But it's possible it was he?"

"Possible? I suppose most things are. But it isn't sense. If it were he, it must have been either murder or suicide.

"I don't say he hadn't some motive for committing suicide, but would anyone choose such a method? And what about Blinkwell having seen him in the lounge a few minutes before? And of Wilkes being in charge of the furnace?

"And it isn't as if we didn't know that the taxi driver had been thrown in an hour or two earlier. And who should want to murder

Snacklit? It's just trying to be too clever, and substituting a wild improbability for a reasonable explanation that fits the facts like a glove."

"Well, I've nothing to say against that. There are only two things that interest me about it now. The one is whether Irene or I will be required to give evidence, and the second is what's going to happen to Blinkwell."

"We're not going to ask you to give evidence. You're clear out of it, so far as our police (or the Sûreté for that matter) are concerned. We can't avoid Irene going into the box. She's one of the most important witnesses, though you can rely on counsel—and the Press—being discreet.

"But as to Blinkwell, I'm afraid I can't do more than pass on the disappointment we're all feeling. We haven't merely decided that we can do nothing ourselves. We've been almost down on our knees begging Paris to look at it in the same way.

"We don't think any magistrate would make an extradition order on Gustav's word, which is the only real evidence they've got. And, for ourselves, we don't feel that we've got sufficient to make a case against him on the drug smuggling issue. We should be just asking for trouble.

"We may be able to look at it rather differently when we've got Snacklit. He'll probably talk in an effort to get himself out of the mess. But, even then there's the same difficulty as with Gustav. It's just a criminal's word, and not much use without better confirmation.

"Still I should say that, if we catch Snacklit, we shall soon have the Professor in the same place. Otherwise not. But you can say it's a hundred to one that we'll get him, one way or other, though we may have to go round by another road."

Mr. Thurlow was satisfied by the explanation. He thought that Snacklit was unlikely to elude pursuit, which he knew to be a much more difficult enterprise in England than in his own more spacious and (in some respects) more primitive land. He thought therefore, that Professor Blinkwell's remaining days of liberty would not be long.

We may observe the soundness of the Professor's judgment when he used his foot, with such economy of effort, to put Snacklit in his appropriate place.

As to what *did* happen to Professor Blinkwell, which exemplified the familiar proverb that the pitcher which goes often to the well will get broken at last—that is another story, and must be told at another time.

But it may be recorded here that both Burfoot and Wilkes were convicted and duly hanged. Wilkes, in a last effort to dodge the rope, did tell his solicitors of the manner of Snacklit's end, which those gentlemen communicated to the police, who, without considering Wilkes to be a mirror of exact truth, were inclined to credit it; and the promotion of Inspector Dunchurch, which shortly followed, may have been partly due to this confirmation of the theory to which he had held so stubbornly. But it was decided that it would be impossible to prosecute Professor Blinkwell on the unsupported evidence of a convicted murderer, and Wilkes' anticipation that he would be kept alive to give that testimony proved to be a mistake.

Irene gave evidence, which the Press treated with that voluntary discretion which is the usual consequence of a word from Whitehall or Downing Street, and that she was the daughter of the American Ambassador was not generally known. The Press of the United States, under banner headlines, had more to say, but it was fortunately of the right kind.

Mr. Thurlow, outlining these future events with considerable accuracy in his astute political mind, was feeling content with the world and with those around him. He would have liked to have continued the conversation after coffee was served. But he was a discreet man, and one who knew when silence or withdrawal are positive rather than negative actions. He said that he had matters of urgency with which to deal in his own room.

Irene and her cousin were left alone; and it is obvious that there is no means of knowing what took place afterwards, beyond disclosures which either of them made, which were not of a detailed kind. But much may be inferred from an announcement in *The Times* which Myra read at breakfast only two mornings later:

A marriage has been arranged—

She laid down the paper, looked at her uncle, started to speak, then checked herself. Her rather heavy features resumed their usual immobility. But it cannot be recorded that she looked pleased.

As to Professor Blinkwell, he took no notice at all. His mind had strayed erratically to the moment when he had struck a blow from behind at a man's neck hard enough to make silence certain, and from such an angle that there would be little risk of any bloodstain resulting upon a dinner jacket which it would have been a pity to spoil.

ABOUT THE AUTHOR

SYDNEY FOWLER WRIGHT (1874-1965) penned over seventy volumes of science fiction, fantasy, classic mysteries, historical novels, poetry, and non-fiction, many of them being published by the Borgo Press Imprint of Wildside Press.